Please

This book contains **<u>EXTREMELY</u>** dark themes that
<u>WILL</u> be distressing to some readers.

Tasting Clementine is filled with dark and disturbing
activities/relationships depicted in graphic detail from the
start.

Please do not take this warning lightly.

You can visit www.hollybloomauthor.com to read the full
and detailed content warnings before reading beyond this
point.

Tasting Clementine

THE VANTA COLLECTION

HOLLY BLOOM

CHAPTER 1

August

"CLEMMIE..."

My voice trails off as she climbs on top of me. Her skinny ass points up as her bikini straps slip down her shoulders. Goddamn, her hard nipples taunt me through the shiny silver fabric. I'd give anything to suck on those pearly-pink pebbles until she moans my name. After I saw her changing, her perfect fucking tits are all I've been able to think about. Them, and the rest of her tight little body. It's no accident I saw her either. She makes a habit of changing as soon as she hears my footsteps in the hall.

She likes me watching.

She wants me to.

Clemmie's wet tongue licks down my chest in a straight line, but her giant green eyes stay fixed on mine. Her stare is vibrant and wild, illuminated by the blue flecks around her irises. No one can deny that she's fucking hot. My cock strains under the fabric, ignoring my brain telling me this is wrong. This shouldn't be happening. Yet, I can't control myself.

"Clemmie, I told you to stop!" I say, more firmly th

time. As firm as a guy with a raging boner can be. "Don't you fucking listen?"

She giggles like it's a game, but I'm not playing around. She's my stepsister. It's wrong, no matter how good she looks or how much I want her. We may not have grown up together, but I knew she needed a brother to protect her from the moment we met. I refuse to be like the others.

"If you wanted me to stop," she says in a playful sing-song way that makes me want to ram my cock down her throat to silence her, "you wouldn't be so hard for me, would you?"

"I can't control it," I hiss, unable to decide whether I'm more turned on or ashamed. How is it possible to feel those two things at once? "What do you expect to happen when you go and act like that?"

We're still wet from swimming in the pool. Her skin glitters from the water, and droplets catch the light, making her sparkle. Going for a midnight swim with Clementine was a bad idea, but it's become our nightly ritual since I moved in with her and our father last summer. It's easy to see why Clemmie is fucked up after living with him.

I was lucky to get away. My parents had a brief romance. Mom moved in with him, but they separated a month after I was born, and we never looked back. Dad remarried a few years later, another blonde junkie just like Mom. When his new wife died suddenly, he was left with her three-year-old daughter from a previous relationship. *Clemmie*. He's the only father she's ever known... and he's a monster.

When I can't sleep, I question whether Clemmie will go the same way as my mom: dying in a state of perpetual bliss with a syringe stuck in her vein, but Clemmie doesn't need drugs to get high. She's never been part of the real world and doesn't want to be.

Clemmie pauses and pouts. My dick rubs against my shorts, taunted by her pussy only a few inches away. All she has to do is slide down a little further. If she brushes against me, I'll be gone and won't be able to hold myself back, but I have to. Fuck, I have to.

"What's wrong?" Her eyes fill with tears. From her reaction, you'd think that I'd slapped her. I should have. Being nice is what got me into this fucking situation. Coming to the pool house is a habit I should break. "Is something wrong with me?"

"There's nothing wrong with you." I reach to pull her close. My instinct to stop her pain overrides the rational side of my brain in a flash. My chest aches at the thought of hurting her, but she pushes me away and jumps up. The wet slap of her feet on the tiles echoes around the room as she marches to a deckchair. She flops down and brings her knees to her chest, refusing to look at me. "Don't be like that, Clemmie. Come back and sit with me."

Her head jerks in my direction, noticing how I say *with* me, not *on* me.

"No!" she snaps, narrowing her eyes. A wild crazy stirs behind them. "Stay away from me."

I should heed her warning.

"Look, it's not that I don't want to..."

I stand and start to walk to where she's sitting, awkwardly shuffling to disguise my hard-on. I'm kidding no one. She looks even more fuckable when she's in a sulk. Clemmie is a psycho, but she hypnotized me from the moment I laid eyes on her. She's cast a spell on me that I can't break.

"You're a tease," she explodes, rising from her chair. She

saunters toward me, and a smug smile spreads over her face. She knows how to push my buttons, so whatever comes out of her mouth next will make me want to choke the life out of her. "If you won't fuck me, Daddy's friends will."

I see red.

I fly at her and grab her by the throat. Unfortunately for her, it's not an even match. I'm six-five and tower over her tiny five-foot frame. I wrap my hand around her neck, and my fingers tightly grip her ghostly pale skin. I use all my strength to slam her back against the wall with a crash. She gurgles as I yank her into the air, forcing the tips of her toes to graze the floor.

"You want them to fuck you, huh?" I demand, spraying her with my spit and fury. "Do you enjoy it when he makes you fuck them one after the other? All those sixty-year-old guys? Do you enjoy them coming inside you? Shooting your used pussy up with their dirty fucking loads?"

Clemmie's grin widens. She isn't afraid. Her cheeks flush from the lack of air, but she manages to laugh.

"Yes," she replies breathily. "Real men aren't afraid of fucking me."

This is what she wants. She wants me to fuck her so badly that she'll push me to do it, but I won't. Not like this. No matter how much I want to. I can't. I care too much about her to do that. Clemmie is part of me. I felt it as soon as we met; we share an invisible tie that I never want to break.

"They're old!" I snarl, releasing my hold on her. "They're so old that they need pills to stay hard."

She strokes the angry red marks I've left on her neck. I didn't squeeze hard enough to bruise, but even if I did, it wouldn't be worse than the bruises she's had before.

"You're older than me," Clemmie says, "and *you* want to fuck me."

"You don't know that I'm older than you, Clemmie. We were born on the same day," I remind her with a scowl. Being born on the same day is a creepy coincidence. Sometimes I wonder whether it explains why the thought of existing without her seems impossible. "What they do to you is sick. How long has *he* been letting them treat you like that?"

Clemmie plays with her hair, and it swishes around her waist. It's dirty blonde, just like Mom's, but it's poker-straight compared to my mother's messy waves. If I stare at her long enough, I can almost imagine she's actually my little sister. The two long braids grazing her shoulders make her look younger than seventeen.

"Are you going to try and get Daddy in trouble?" she asks, then tuts. "You've never liked him."

Whether I like him or not has nothing to do with it. Our father is a sadistic motherfucker. I'm only here because Mom died a month before my seventeenth birthday, and he agreed to take me in. If Clemmie hadn't refused to leave with me, I'd have run away from this weird-ass gothic mansion months ago. I know how to take care of myself. We turn eighteen in a few weeks, and I don't know what will happen next. All I do know is that I can't let her go.

When I first arrived, I couldn't believe how different our lives were. Mom and I lived in a rundown trailer on grilled cheese sandwiches while Clemmie and Dad were loaded. Our father earned his fortune by investing in tech companies and bought this house when Clemmie was a kid. She never went to school. He kept her here and treated her like his personal Barbie, but this is no Malibu fucking dream house.

"How long, Clemmie?" I press her for answers.

I found out about the parties a month after I moved in. I watched through the peepholes and saw what they did to her. A group of older men sharing a teenage girl is one thing, but what disturbed me more was how much she liked it. The whore rode their cocks with a smile like she was bouncing on a Hoppity Hop. As I watched, I came in my pants, imagining it was my cock she was riding.

That was the start of it all.

"I don't know!" She rolls her eyes and exhales dramatically. "It doesn't matter."

"It matters to me."

"You're getting jealous. August's getting jealous! August's getting jealous!" Her chanting bounces off the walls, filling the space, but she doesn't stop. "August's getting jealous!"

"Shut up!" I blast.

If she spoke any louder, she could wake him. If Dad found us down here alone, he wouldn't be happy. He likes keeping her locked up like a prisoner. His prisoner.

She wiggles her eyebrows. "Make me."

"I'm being serious."

"August's getting jealous!" she continues, the volume rising. "August's getting jealous!"

I run and push her into the pool, then tumble in after her with a giant splash. She emerges from the water like a goddess.

"Oops!" She giggles and points to her floating bikini top across the water's surface. "I've lost something."

I gulp and keep my eyes fixed on her face. I shouldn't feel this way, but...

"You can look if you want," she offers.

"I've already told you." My jaw tenses with resolve,

although I'm not sure how much more self-control I have left. It's the same every time we're alone. She chips away at me, and I'm getting to a point where I will not be able to resist for much longer. "We can't—"

Clemmie dives underwater so she doesn't have to listen to the end of my sentence. Seconds later, her hands tug at my swim shorts and pull them down. I kick her away, but she moves like a mermaid beneath me.

This is bad.

She comes up for air in hysterical laughter, then spits water like a fountain. She grins and says, "Now we're even. We've both lost something."

"That's not funny, Clemmie."

I pull up my shorts, and her face turns solemn. Her stare burns into my skin, making it prickle. I could get lost in her eyes for days. She will destroy both of our fucking souls if I let her.

"You have a nice cock," she says casually like she's complimenting my sweet new ride or how I style my hair.

Blood rushes to my groin, and the head of my cock swells at her approval. I've never had complaints from other girls I've slept with, but it means more coming from her.

"Why do you always turn everything back to sex?" I snap.

"Sex is everything," she replies, swimming gracefully to the deep end and treading water. "Don't you know anything?"

"You're wrong," I say, following her. I don't need to swim. I'm tall enough to reach the bottom. "There's more to life than sex."

"Sex makes you feel good."

"What Dad makes those men do to you isn't good," I point out. "They're using you."

"Why do you have to be so mean all the time?" She splashes me. "They like me. They want me!"

"They want to *fuck* you," I correct her. "There's a difference."

"What makes you any different?"

I should leave the pool. Things have gotten complicated fast. I should head straight for a cold shower and jack off to the thought of how good it would feel to bury myself inside her, but I stay. I'm not like the other men in her life. I want to protect her.

"I care about you," I say, choosing my words carefully. "Fucking is about more than feeling good. If you love someone, sex feels better."

She floats on her back now, extending her arms wide at her sides. Her breasts break the surface of the water like small peaks. She hasn't been socialized to feel self-conscious about being naked. Her openness with her body is refreshing, but it also makes me fucking furious. Dad made her this way. He wants her to be unashamed and ready to share herself with anyone he presents. I don't want her showing herself to everyone. Those saggy-balled fuckers don't deserve to jizz over her perfection. She doesn't realize how beautiful she is, but those twisted fuckers do. Fucking her is the closest they'll get to heaven because they're going straight to hell.

Clementine Jackson is a fucking angel. My angel.

"An orgasm is an orgasm," Clemmie says. She's immature in many ways but extremely adult in others, like how she candidly talks about sex. Another thing I have to thank our sack of shit father for. "They always feel good."

"Sex can mean something too."

I usually try to avoid this topic of conversation and ask her about the books she reads. To my knowledge, reading is all she does between the weekly parties. Sometimes she asks me about my job at the garage. Fixing cars is easy. It's something I've always been good at. There was a garage outside the trailer park where I grew up, and the owner let me work there. He never paid me for my work but would give me hotdogs or bags of chips in exchange. I didn't give a shit about child labor laws if it meant getting something to eat. Helping rebuild cars was a lifeline to me. It kept me out of trouble and kept me away from my mom.

She was a drug addict who kicked her son out of the trailer to service guys to put more junk in her body. Like Clemmie, sex meant nothing to her. Maybe Dad made her that way too. Mom never spoke about him, and now I finally understand why.

"I don't believe you," Clemmie says. "How many girls have you slept with?"

My cock softens at the thought of the women I got hot and heavy with in the past. Having sex at thirteen was normal where I'm from. Getting pregnant before sixteen was practically a rite of passage. Thankfully I got lucky. Most girls I fucked were older and couldn't afford another kid. I've always looked older, and the women I fucked never asked questions when they invited me inside.

After losing my virginity, I stopped going to school altogether. I could read and write but didn't see the point in traveling an hour to get there. Why did I need to study when I could fix cars and get paid? Besides, the authorities didn't bother checking up on me and assumed we had skipped town.

"Twenty," I say.

The actual number is half that, but I don't want to make her feel bad.

"Do you know how many people I've had sex with?" she asks. "Guess."

"The same as me?"

She laughs. "More."

My stomach lurches. "How many more?"

"I don't know exactly, a couple hundred, maybe more," she says like it's nothing. I want to kill every motherfucker who hurt her. "Sometimes it's the same people, other times it's different ones. They all blur into one. Sex is just sex. It's no big deal. That's what Daddy says."

"Daddy doesn't know what he's talking about," I snarl. "You shouldn't listen to him."

Since her childhood, he's primed her to spread her legs. He's taught her that she must please men. She sees it as a privilege.

"He said I shouldn't listen to you!" She flips over onto her front and swims toward me. "Why should I?"

"Because I haven't left yet," I say.

Her face falls, and the light atmosphere between us disappears.

"You're not still planning on going, are you?" she whispers. "It's our birthday in a few weeks."

"I'm not leaving you here," I say, dropping my voice. Even though we're alone and this is one of the only places on the property not covered by cameras, I fear what will happen if Dad finds out we've spoken about this. He'd lock her in her bedroom until she was too old to satisfy his twisted appetites. "I want you to come with me."

"I've already told you," she says. "I can't leave Daddy. He needs me."

I want to tell her that the bastard can rot and die for all I care, but I don't know how she'll react. Until I showed up, he was the only person she's ever cared about, and he's brainwashed her into believing that no one else will be there for her like he is.

A clock chime rings to remind us that it's two a.m. Time we should leave.

I stroke her cheek, forgetting she's topless. "Just think about it, okay?"

She doesn't reply but inclines her head.

Is that a yes?

"I need you to say it," I say. "Promise me you'll think about it."

"I promise," she whispers, then sinks, leaving only bubbles behind.

The next thing I know, she's climbing out and wrapping a towel around her middle.

"Sweet dreams, August," she chirps. "Don't let the bed bugs bite."

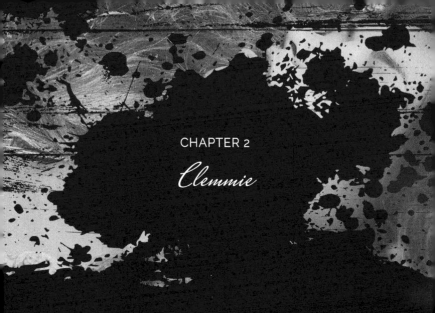

CHAPTER 2

Clemmie

DADDY WORKS HARD. HE ALWAYS HAS.

I make him breakfast just the way he likes it. Oatmeal, black coffee, two slices of toast—a light brown color with a thin spread of butter, and strawberry jam on Mondays and Sundays as a treat. He says you have to start and end the week in the best way.

I've been thinking about what August said last night. He doesn't understand how things work here. I hoped he'd get it the longer he stayed. I thought he might even come to Daddy's parties; maybe then he'd fully appreciate how the men worship me there.

I'm not stupid. I know he watches and has seen what happens. I like to give him a show, and I think of him when I'm fucking them. None of them are like him.

August was right about them being old, though. They're all three times my age, at least. Some of them are attractive, but others aren't. Daddy told me it doesn't matter what I think. They pay good money to have me. Whatever they demand, I have to do it. It's my job. Daddy does so much for me, and it's only fair I give something back.

"Morning, Daddy," I say as I carry the breakfast tray into his bedroom.

I love our house. It's filled with old-fashioned furniture, red carpet, and wood-paneled walls. August thinks it's creepy, but I think it's beautiful. It's not like the rest of the world. Things are different here. We don't have to worry about what's going on out there.

"Clementine." Daddy smiles from under his sheets. "Good morning."

Daddy is a handsome man. He's in his late fifties and in good shape. He's tall but not as tall as August, and they share the same timeless gray eyes.

"Do you want me to put the tray on your lap?" I ask.

"Put it on the side," he instructs.

"Yes, Daddy."

I do as he requests, placing it carefully on top of the wooden chest at the back of the room. A chest filled with secrets. Some of them even I don't know. I've never looked inside without him around. He carries the key to the lock on a chain around his neck and only opens it on special occasions.

He pats the spot on the bed next to him. "Why don't you come and sit with me?"

"Of course, Daddy."

I climb onto his big four-poster. When I was younger, I remember thinking this bed was fit for a princess.

"I want to talk to you about your birthday," he says. "Eighteen means you're becoming an adult now. A woman."

My heart races. Does he know about my conversation

with August last night? I've always been careful. We sneak past all the external cameras on our way out. I know every inch of this place. I'm not sure why the thought of him learning about our time in the pool house makes me so nervous. There's nothing wrong with spending time alone with my new brother, but something tells me to stay quiet. I don't like it when Daddy's unhappy.

I lean back into the plump cushions.

I'm wearing a floral dress with strappy sleeves. It's the same blue and white as old china with a similar intricate pattern. It's supposed to be short, but my height makes everything longer than it should be, and it sits around my knees.

Daddy's hand rises from beneath the comforter. He slides under the hem of my dress to stroke my thigh, and I tense without realizing it.

"Clementine." My slight movement doesn't go unnoticed, and his voice is firm. Commanding. "What's wrong?"

"Nothing, Daddy," I say, parting my legs wider to show him I'm fine. "I'm just not feeling well this morning."

It's a lie. I'm feeling better than ever. Being around August does that to me. Ever since he moved in, something changed. I don't live for the parties but for spending time with him—even if he does like to tease me mercilessly.

I've never wanted to fuck a man so badly as I do August. I feel like a balloon is in my chest. It grows the longer we spend together and makes me feel like I might just burst. He wants me back. I know he does. Maybe even more than I want him, but he fights it. He can't deny that he wants me much longer. The longer he resists, the harder he struggles with it.

It's different with August. I didn't need to ask who he was when he showed up that night. The similarities between him and Daddy were obvious, and I always knew Daddy had a son who was taken away by an evil woman. When I saw him, I finally felt like our family was complete. Although, I'd feel more complete if he fucked me.

Daddy's hand moves further up my thigh, squeezing my flesh, then pulls out suddenly from under my dress. His fingers go to rub the key on his neck.

"I know something that'll make you feel better," he murmurs.

My pussy starts to flutter with excitement.

"But Daddy," I say, "it's not a special day."

"It's the first day of summer, Clementine," Daddy says. "What could be any more special than a new season?"

He gets out of bed and strides to the chest, moving his breakfast tray to the floor. His food will go cold, but I keep my mouth shut, not wanting to distract him from opening his special chest.

I love the noise it makes when it clicks open. I crane my neck to peek inside, but I see nothing behind Daddy's shoulders. He moves items around, scanning his collection. These treasures aren't the stuff downstairs or the ones he sells. These are custom-built for me. Daddy is an intelligent man. He certainly knows how to make good machines.

"Ah, yes," he mumbles. A few seconds later, he takes out an item. "This will do nicely."

I crawl to the edge of the bed to get a better look at what he's holding in his hands. "What is it, Daddy?"

I squint and frown. It's different from his usual implements. They're usually colorful and curved or metal, like the clamps and spreaders. I'm not sure where this one is going to go. It looks like an oxygen mask from a hospital show, but smaller.

"This is going to make you feel really good, Clementine," Daddy reassures, approaching the bed again. His eyes shine the same way August's do, and I get wetter thinking about August's cock bobbing in the pool. Whenever I think of him, I can't help getting turned on. "Be a good girl and lay back for Daddy. Put your head on the pillow and pull up your dress for me."

I do as he asks, hoisting it to expose my red panties. They're an expensive brand. One of Daddy's friends bought them for me to wear.

"What about my panties?" I ask.

"Take them off too."

I slowly roll them down to expose my pussy. I've been getting waxed ever since I started getting hair down there. Daddy's friend used to do it. He liked coming to see me until the hair stopped growing back. Daddy was angry at him when the visits stopped, but I didn't mind. He gave me wax burns once, and after that, I became apprehensive.

I sink into the bed. It's the most comfortable mattress in the world. A big fluffy soft cloud. It's been a while since I played with Daddy. I was beginning to think he was getting tired of me, but I haven't minded since August has entertained me.

Daddy pulls a chair over to the side of the bed.

"Good girl, Clementine," he says. "Now turn around to face me so Daddy can get a better view of your pussy."

I swivel, taking the pillow with me, and spread my legs. He chuckles as he places the unfamiliar mask over my mound. A black tube comes off of it like a telephone wire, and it has a shiny beetle-like vibrator in the center that nestles against my clit. Two wires run from it to a remote and bulb Daddy holds in his hands.

"This is a pump," he explains. He squeezes the round black bulb, which causes a strange suction-like sensation.

The sucking secures the sides of the mask tightly in place. "This is going to make you feel better. You'll see."

I'm not sure how I feel about it until he presses another button, and the gentle buzz of the vibrator makes me relax. That's a sensation I'm familiar with.

"Good girl," he purrs. "Just relax."

I close my eyes and gasp in surprise as the pump continues stealing my air like it's trying to vacuum seal my pussy. Instead, I focus on the buzzing against my clit and let my mind wander to August. I think of his golden skin and taut muscles, his calloused hands from working on cars, and his forehead slicked with grease when he gets home from work. I watch him return from my bedroom window every day. He never gets out of the car straight away, choosing to sit outside like he can't believe he's here.

"Look at how big your pussy is getting," Daddy gushes.

I open my eyes and look down to see him peering between my legs, watching through the clear Perspex in fascination. His hot breath tickles my thighs, and the pumping intensifies. I moan, unable to contain myself. I'm wet from thinking about August, and my wetness is starting to collect in the cup.

I watch my usually small lips fill the Perspex, growing in size and getting pinker. A wave of pleasure races through me from the combination of sensations and vibrations.

"Would you like more?" Daddy asks.

"Yes," I breathe, writhing on the bed and gripping the sheets. "I need more."

"Yes, what?"

I yelp as the vibrating bullet stops, leaving me suspended on the edge. My hips gyrate furiously, wanting to chase the high. Where are my manners?

"Yes, please, Daddy," I moan obediently. "I need more."

"Good girl," he answers.

His approval turns me on, and the buzzing resumes at a higher intensity. My blood rushes between my legs, making every little stroke more pronounced. I start to shake. It's beginning to be painful, but I don't want it to stop as I squeeze my breasts. I never wear a bra in the house, and my nipples stand to attention under my dress. I pinch them hard. I want my pussy to be filled but can't get to it, so playing with my nipples will have to do.

My thighs tremble as I come hard. I cry out as my pussy contracts and releases, spraying the inside of the Perspex with my sticky heat. There's nowhere else for it to go. I'm a squirter. It's something Daddy's friends like about me. I can't help it. It just happens!

"Are you starting to feel better, Clementine?" Daddy asks.

"Yes!" The constant sucking is getting more uncomfortable, but I won't complain. I know better than that. Daddy does things on his terms, but he notices my wincing and takes pity on me.

He removes the pump with a pop, then puts the mask to his lips and tips it back to drink my juices. He licks his lips after he swallows and winks. "That's Daddy's favorite breakfast."

"Daddy!" I gawp at the engorged pulsing horror between my legs. My pussy has quadrupled in size. My lips rub against my inner thighs, and my clit is so ginormous that it could wear a hat. "Will it stay like this?"

"Don't worry, Clemmie," he reassures me, stroking my knee. "It'll go back to normal soon."

I sigh in relief, but my giant pussy refuses to be ignored. It craves attention, and now I know my bulbous lips won't stay this way forever. I look at them with a newfound interest.

Daddy reaches under the bed to retrieve a bottle of lube. He squirts the slippery gel over my pussy, but he doesn't touch me. He is as intrigued as I am by my new appearance, and his fingers knead my inner thighs gently.

"It's okay, Clemmie," he says. "You can touch yourself for Daddy. I know you want to."

Thank fuck for that. With his permission granted, I eagerly reach down to stroke my swollen flesh and smear the lube all over, not that I need it. I only have to brush over my clit to shiver in delight. I plunge three fingers inside myself. It feels good to pump them in and out, but they are not enough. They don't quench my desperate need to be filled.

"Daddy." I bat my eyelashes at him. He likes that. "Pretty please, can I have some more?"

He goes to his chest to retrieve one of my favorites. A curved crystal dildo that hits all the right places. "How about this?"

"Fuck yes!" I say. "I mean, yes, please, Daddy."

He hands it over and returns to his spot to watch as I ram the dildo inside my wet hole and squeal. Daddy gets his phone and starts recording. I think nothing of it. This moment should be captured. My pussy looks like a blooming pink flower.

"There's a good girl," Daddy encourages, "fuck yourself just like that. Show your fat pussy to the camera for all our friends."

I extract it with a squelch. Wetness trickles down my legs and soaks the sheets. Daddy doesn't say anything, so he mustn't mind. We don't usually play upstairs. He prefers it when we're in our entertaining space.

"Look at that," Daddy says. He holds the camera real close to capture every dripping detail. He uses his other hand to make a V-shape with his fingers and spreads me open, making me writhe under his touch. My clit pulses so violently that I can see it moving. "Now, make yourself come for the camera like a good girl."

I don't hesitate, guiding the dildo inside myself and using my spare hand to rub my clit.

I don't hear the footsteps outside until it's too late, and the door flies open.

August stands in the doorway. His hands ball into fists, and his jaw is clenched. Seeing him catapults me into a dizzying orgasm, and I stare into his gray eyes as my wetness coats the glass.

Daddy puts his phone down as I continue to moan.

"August," Daddy greets him coldly, "what are you doing here?"

August eyeballs my pussy like it's a monster and spits, "What have you done to her?"

I snap my knees together. The sudden movement makes my clit sting from the increased sensitivity, but it feels so good that I can't help another loud moan escaping my lips.

August's lip curls in disapproval, and Daddy's expression darkens.

"You should knock before coming in," Daddy warns.

"It'll..." I stammer between breathy gasps as my pussy spasms over the dildo, "go back to normal soon."

"We were about to talk about your birthday," Daddy says, "as soon as Clementine feels better."

I'm a hell of a lot better now.

"I'll come back later," August snarls, then slams the door shut behind him.

My heart sinks in disappointment. The only thing that would have made breakfast even better was if he was the one filling me.

CHAPTER 3

August

I WANT TO KILL HIM.

I keep seeing her over and over again. I wasn't able to concentrate at work with the image of her burned into my retinas. *My Clementine.* My perfect girl spread wide open with bulging red lips. Her moans rocked my core as I watched her wetness drip down her thighs. How am I supposed to control my urges when I can't stop wondering whether she tastes as sweet as her name?

I don't know what fucked-up shit Dad did to her to make her like that. He should be protecting her, not making her soak his fucking sheets. The worst thing is that I'm not sure whether I'm more furious at him for what he does or jealous that I'm not the one who has a front-row seat.

Does that make me as bad as him?

No. I care about what happens to her, and I've fought my urges. I want to protect her from him. I don't want anyone else to hurt her again. Everything I do is for her, even if she doesn't realize it.

Everyone treats Clemmie like a toy, but she's so much

more than that. I'll need to work hard to get her away from this place. It's the only way we stand a chance.

I wait for her in the pool house, but I'm unsure whether she'll show up. It's past midnight, and I pace back and forth in the shadows like a wild animal. What will I say when I see her? It's one thing to know what he subjects her to at the parties he throws for his sick bunch of friends, but it's another to realize it happens in his bed too.

My head spins around as hinges creak.

There she is.

Clemmie walks in wearing her pretty sundress. The same dress bunched around her waist to show off her milky thighs earlier. Under the moonlight, she looks innocent, like Alice lost in Wonderland. She clicks the door closed and stands still. The silver glow hits her perfectly, displaying her rosy-pink nipples hiding underneath the floral fabric.

"August," she says, playing with her braid. "I didn't know whether you'd be here tonight."

I'm torn between pinning her against the wall and railing her to release my building frustration or reassuring her that everything will be okay. I go with the latter.

"Why?" I ask gently. "Because of what I saw earlier?"

She shrugs, biting her lip.

"Clemmie..." I approach her, and she doesn't move. "He's supposed to be your dad. You know it's wrong, don't you? What he does to you isn't normal."

How is it possible to be within touching distance but still feel like the gap between us is miles apart?

"Daddy loves me, August." Her eyes widen. "He'll do anything for me. He only wants the best for me."

My shoulders shake with rage. I inhale deeply to steady myself before I lose my shit, then say, "He's a monster."

"Shh," she soothes, stroking my forearm. "Did you fix a lot of cars today?"

I blink in disbelief.

How can she go from one subject to another so fast?

"Yeah," I murmur.

Clemmie slips off her sandals and goes to sit by the edge of the pool. She dangles her feet over the side and into the water, then asks, "How did you learn to fix cars?"

"Where… I used to live… there was a place nearby," I say. I'm struggling to let go of my anger but focus on answering her question. "A guy taught me."

"Can you teach me one day?"

"You want to fix cars?" I raise an eyebrow and grin. "Since when?"

"Why not? I'd get to work with you all day," she says gleefully, "maybe we could start a business together."

"We could," I say, kneeling to unlace my sneakers and take my socks off. I sit next to her, dipping my feet into the cool water. "But we can only do that if we leave here. We're eighteen soon. We can go anywhere we want. Start over."

"I'm not sure I'd like to go somewhere else," she says. "This home is all I know. I like it here. It has everything I need."

From our previous conversations, I know that Clemmie can't remember leaving the mansion's grounds. She's learned everything she knows about the world from reading books or watching television.

"I'll show you the real world, Clemmie," I promise. "I'll show you there's more to it than this house and these gardens. More than the parties. There's a whole fucking world waiting for you to discover it. Wouldn't you like to go to the places you've read about?"

"I've read about them, August," she talks like I'm a

stupid child who knows nothing. "Why would I need to go there too? Look what happened to your mom when she left."

I've told her about what happened. My mom may have spent most of her life high until a third overdose took her life, but it still beats being here with him.

"You're not her," I say. "She was an addict. She had a problem."

Clemmie scowls. "Did you love her like I love Daddy?"

"No," I growl. "I hated the bitch."

Clemmie giggles and covers her mouth, kicking her feet to spray water over us.

"Hey, quit it!"

She ignores me, kicks the surface again, and then says, "You shouldn't have left earlier. I wanted you to stay."

"I couldn't," I mumble, averting my gaze to the tiles shifting in appearance under the water. "I couldn't watch."

"I was thinking about you," she says. "When I was—"

"I saw what you were doing," I interrupt. "I don't need a fucking play-by-play."

Her small hand creeps onto my lap, and she threads her fingers through mine.

"Come on," she says, "let's swim!"

She tugs hard and pulls us both in fully clothed.

"Clemmie!" I flip my hair out of my face. I'm standing in the deep end of the pool, and the water comes to my shoulders. "What the fuck was that?"

She throws her head back and laughs. Her laugh is like a tinkling wind chime; it's contagious and carries through the air. She swims forward. Her dress floats around her like a strange jellyfish, and she comes to me. Her arms cling to mine, and she wraps her legs around my torso underwater.

"Have you felt like this about someone before?" she

asks. I try my hardest to ignore how good her body feels and keep my arms pressed to my sides. "You know, like the way you feel about me?"

She looks like a china doll with high cheekbones and pouty lips. She reminds me of Mom before she resigned herself to a life of starvation and heroin. Dad has a type. A strand of wet hair falls over her face.

"Of course not," I say, brushing the hair out of her eyes. "It's different with you, Clemmie."

"You may not want to face your thoughts, but I can see them," she murmurs, pressing her tits tightly against my chest.

"I think we need to get you out of those wet clothes before you freeze to death."

I carry her and wade through the water, placing her firmly on the side. There's underfloor heating in the pool house, but the temperature drops at night. Plus, I can't have her rubbing against me much longer.

"Fine," she relents, getting out. The wet fabric hugs every delicious curve of her body. "Have it your way."

I avert my eyes as she pulls her dress over her head but cast a glance as she strolls to a stack of dry towels wearing nothing but her lace panties. She knows I'm watching. She walks slower, and her hips sway with confidence beyond her years.

"Maybe we should warm up in the sauna?" she suggests, finally wrapping a towel around herself and tipping her head toward a door. Dad has more money than sense. Clemmie may have been locked up for most of her life, but at least it was a five-star fucking prison.

"Fine," I growl.

Before hauling myself out of the water, I wait until she disappears into the steamy, red-lit room. I peel off my shirt, step out of my shorts, and head to the sauna in my boxers.

I walk into a wall of heat.

"Holy fuck," I exhale. "It's hot."

It's been a while since I've experienced heat like this. It reminds me of spending summers in the trailer without AC.

"I like it in here," Clemmie says.

I sit next to her, and the scorching wood burns the back of my thighs.

Clemmie's eyes are closed, and her arms sprawl across the slats. If the heat didn't make me short of breath, the sight of her topless would. I look between her thighs, relieved to see her pussy appears to be a normal size again.

"I told you it would go back," she says with a smile.

Fuck. I didn't realize that she had opened her eyes again.

"You shouldn't be messing with shit like that," I huff, crossing my arms.

She shuffles closer. The heat catches in my throat, and beads of sweat form over our skin. Her thigh touches mine and sends an electric shock straight to my cock. It takes me off guard, and my head is spinning so hard that I don't stop her from taking my hand.

"See?" Clemmie whispers, placing my hand between her legs. "I'm fine. It didn't hurt. It felt good."

I should yank my hand away, but she forces my fingers to stroke the front of her panties. She's already wet, and the fabric is slick. An invitation for more. She holds me there and pushes her hips against me. She moans before I realize what she's doing.

"You feel so good," she murmurs. I want to play with her, but I know I shouldn't. "Mmm."

"This isn't—"

"Please, August," she begs, grinding against my palm. "I want you to make me feel good."

As my rational brain kicks in, I try to pull myself away, but she pushes my hand back. I'm strong enough to over-power her, but the pleading look in her eyes makes me stay. "We shouldn't be doing this."

"Stay," she urges, rocking against me. Her pussy swells in desire, and the thin fabric disappears into her wet slit, allowing me to feel her silky outer lips as she rolls against me. "Please, just a little longer..."

This isn't the same as me touching her, right? Her cheeks flush as she sighs and continues to move against my fingers.

"Yes," she moans. "That feels so fucking good."

I want to slide her panties to the side, slip into her wetness, and taste her sweet juices, but I don't move. Her stare meets mine, and I'm fucking mesmerized. We're trans-fixed on each other as she continues to move and pleasure herself against me.

"August!" she cries my name as she comes undone.

Holy fuck. I've never been so turned on before. What does that make me? Does it make me as bad as the others? Does it make me as bad as Dad?

While her chest is still heaving, I yank my hand out of her grasp.

"Where are you going?" she calls after me as I storm away.

I don't answer.

CHAPTER 4

Clemmie

I CAN'T SLEEP AND ROCK MY HIPS AGAINST THE pillow to chase away the emptiness August left in my pussy. His fingers felt even better than I imagined, but he ran away.

How good would it feel if he touched me of his own accord? My thighs tense and quake as I rub my throbbing clit against the cushion until I come over the thought of him.

I expect he's back in his bedroom, wallowing like he always does. He doesn't understand how good we have it. We don't speak much in the main house, preferring to talk in the pool house at night when we can be alone.

August almost stopped resisting today. I could sense it. I wanted him to let go of his worries more than I've ever wanted anything, but he is too controlled in his actions. He had to be growing up with his awful mother who kept him from us. The only good thing to come from her was August —even then, Daddy isn't fond of his son. Maybe it's because he reminds him of the person he used to be.

The early morning sun streams through the gap in the

curtains. We have a party to look forward to this evening. It won't be as good as the special event Daddy is planning for our birthday. He told me it would be a surprise, and he will buy me something special. Butterflies flutter in my stomach at the prospect.

There's a knock on my door, and I jolt upright.

A voice comes from the other side, "Clemmie?"

I smooth down my hair and roll out of bed, wearing an oversized T-shirt that drowns me. It's white and thin, so thin that my nipples are visible.

I push the door ajar, raise a finger to my lips to quieten him, and whisper, "What are you doing here?"

Daddy will be in his workshop at this hour, busy working on his computer or inventions. As well as making the best toys on the planet, he's building a website that'll change the world. I don't understand the details. He says I don't have to. A pretty girl like me doesn't have to think about things like that. All that matters is that I know how to part my legs on request.

August edges inside, slipping through the gap. For someone large, he can creep like a giant cat. I click the door shut behind us and start to speak, but his rough hand muffles my mouth.

"Shh," he purrs. "I want you to listen, not talk. Do you understand?"

I smell him—earthy, oil-stained hands from hard work and something else. I can't describe it, but one sniff is enough to make my panties wet again. I want to breathe him in, savor his scent, and let it consume me.

My head is dizzy, but I nod in understanding, and he takes his hand away. I put two fingers to my mouth and make a zipping motion to show I'll be quiet. His gaze lingers on my chest, and his Adam's apple bobs in longing.

Why do we have to talk when there are better uses for our mouths? I hope he's come to apologize for his rudeness last night.

"I want you to leave with me now," he says in a low, menacing tone. "I'll get the car ready. We don't have to take anything with us. We'll go far away from here and won't look back. I don't want you to go to one of his parties again, Clemmie."

My lips part, but he presses his hand over my mouth again.

"I'll be outside in two hours," he growls. His eyes burn into mine. "Put some clothes on."

I wiggle my eyebrows and look downward to make a point, making him sigh.

"Proper clothes," he corrects himself and continues, "Meet me outside the house, and we'll get out of here—you and me. I'll take us far away, somewhere we can start over. Somewhere we don't have to be Clementine and August Jackson."

But what about Daddy?

"Clemmie, please..." August moves his hand to stroke my hair as if he can read my thoughts. "If you don't go with me, I'm leaving without you."

"I can't go," I whisper, "not yet."

This house is all I know. I've spent my life roaming the long corridors, getting to know every dark corner of the grounds, and learning where the special spots are. It's a beautiful place. Daddy modernized the house, but I begged him to keep some of the original features. I like them. They made me feel like a character in a storybook.

August can't look at me. He leaves without making a sound or stepping on any of the creaky floorboards.

I retrieve my diary from under the mattress and return

to bed. I'm no good at writing. I can never find the right words, but I like to draw. Sketched pictures bring my deepest fantasies to life. Things I'm not sure whether August will understand. He thinks he's done bad things before, but it's nothing compared to what I've done or want to do.

I add details to a medieval torture device. They're one of my favorite things to draw. I giggle at the thought of the guillotine chopping someone's head off and draw a ramp for it to hurtle down before transcending into an open cage of hungry rats. I shade in their jagged little teeth, then chew on the end of my pencil, pondering what other torture I can inflict on what's left of the stick person's body.

August doesn't understand that Daddy keeping me here isn't only for his benefit. He thinks I'm a prisoner, but Daddy gives me a safe environment to explore my urges in exchange for helping his friends.

Time passes, and I rise to look out of the window. August lounges on the hood of his car, looking up at me. There's no one else around. We're in the middle of nowhere. The guests won't arrive until nightfall, and Daddy won't stop working until late.

August's eyes meet mine. I hope he understands. It's a full-length window, and I press my hand against the glass as a peace offering. I might want to leave one day, but I can't... not yet.

I need to give him a reason to stay.

I pull my nightshirt over my head. He doesn't look away as I trail my hands over my breasts, then down to my hips and over my panties. I kneel and blow against the glass, causing it to fog. I use my finger to write 'STAY' as big as possible. It's hard to write backward, but I think I manage it. The message won't last long before it disappears. I stand up and grin, then tug my panties down. The message evaporates with each passing second to reveal more of my pussy.

August's jaw clenches. He turns away and gets into the car. The engine revs as the wheels hurtle away, leaving a spray of gravel and dust behind and my naked frame trembling against the window. I've never felt alone here before, but the thought of him never returning fills me with dread.

Am I not enough for him?

I close the curtains to shut the sunlight out, drawing a deep breath to stop my anger from rising. I dive onto my bed and grab my teddy bear. One I've had for years. I hold its head and squeeze, imagining it's August's neck, and his face is turning purple. I turn the teddy's head, wringing it until his sparse fur stretches and stuffing starts to leak from a hole in the stitches, then I stop.

Killing August would be like killing a part of myself. I couldn't do that.

I smooth the fur, then stroke the bear lovingly. It was a birthday gift from Daddy. He made it just for me. I called him Mr. Darcey.

Mr. Darcey knows all my secrets, the good and evil. He has a hard nose and a snout made from a strange silicone-like material. It's silky against my skin but not cold. There's a switch on his back hidden by the fur. When I turn it on, his nose vibrates. There are different modes to change the speed. I slip Mr. Darcey between my legs and hold his snout to my pussy.

My body responds instantly to the stimulation like I've been taught to, but there's an emptiness to it. Mr. Darcey can't fill the hole August left behind, even if I unzipped his special pouch and pulled out the corkscrew-shaped dildo to fuck myself with. I don't want to wash him today, so his nose will have to do. Besides, my pussy will be filled at the party later.

I come hard and fast. I hold Mr. Darcey in my arms when I'm done, hugging him to my chest. He'll never let me down unless he runs out of batteries.

"What should I do, Mr. D?" I murmur. "Will August come back to me?"

His glassy black eyes stare vacantly, offering zero comfort or words of advice.

"I know you don't care." I sigh. "But what am I meant to do, Mr. Darcey? I can't leave Daddy... I can't leave this place... can I?"

I have no time to feel sorry for myself because there's a knock on my door. I don't bother trying to hide what I'm doing as Daddy walks in without an invitation and sees me cuddling Mr. Darcey.

Daddy smirks. "I see preparations for the evening are underway."

"Yes, Daddy," I say, positioning Mr. Darcey between my legs. His shiny nose and stitched smile grin at him. "We've been playing together."

"Good," Daddy says. The erection in his pants grows, making me feel better instantly. August doesn't appreciate me how Daddy says men should appreciate a woman. August doesn't like the way Daddy and his friends act. "I will see you this evening, Clementine. Don't tire yourself out."

"I won't," I chirp back, knowing Daddy won't spoil me before the party.

At least I have something to look forward to now.

How could she want to stay there? It's hell on fucking earth.

Why does she want to be somewhere where he does those things to her and where he lets his friends treat her like a blow-up doll?

I hit the gas hard and speed down the highway. My knuckles whiten like my bones are gonna tear through the skin from gripping the wheel. I roar at the top of my lungs until my throat hurts like I've eaten gravel.

I *need* to protect her.

I swerve around a few cars ahead, making the tires screech. You should never overtake on a bend, but I do it anyway. Fuck it.

I replay our conversation. I gave Clemmie a mother-fucking out, but she didn't take it. I think back to when I gave Mom a similar chance.

We always struggled for cash when I was a kid. Mom injected any money we had into her veins, apart from the time she managed to stay clean for a few months. She met a guy one summer, and he supported her through her crazy withdrawal while I slept outside our trailer. Things settled after that... until I walked in on him kicking the shit out of her and decided I had to act. Enough was enough.

I grabbed a baseball bat and balaclava, then headed straight to our nearest store. I'm not proud of robbing it or how I cracked the cashier's skull. The cashier was the same age as me, from a good family, and would have plenty of opportunities to make something of himself. A skull fracture would heal, but I needed the money. Mom's life was at stake.

After clearing the register, I had five hundred dollars. It's enough that we could have left town and gotten away from the guy who had turned from her savior into her nemesis, but I didn't think through the next steps properly. Plans didn't matter to a fourteen-year-old. I figured we'd work shit out along the way. We'd be a normal family again. Now she was clean, and the whole world stretched before us... until it didn't.

By the time I cycled back to the trailer park with a backpack stuffed full of cash and a bloody bat, Mom was lying unconscious, and *he* loomed over her body.

"What're you staring at, August?" he snarled. His warm breath smelled of stale beer. "Me and your mom are done."

"It's your fault!" I screamed in his face. "If you hadn't—"

"If I hadn't what, huh?" He yanked my shirt to pull me closer, spraying spit with each word. "You didn't think you could change her, did you? Your mom will always be a junkie whore."

"You're a bastard," I hissed, then he swung at me.

I dodged his punch, but my backpack split in the scuffle and showed him what was inside. Something he didn't want to share.

The fucker beat the shit outta me, took the money, and left us. Things got worse from there. That was the beginning of the end.

If I ever saw him again, I'd kill the fucker. Elias Jacobson deserved to die, but I'd never get close enough. The Jacobson family is untouchable and are well-known in the criminal underworld. He only started fucking my mom because he was her supplier, and I suspected he only got her clean to crush her again. If Elias was anything like his brother Raphael, who is rumored to have a sick appetite for underage girls, I wouldn't put it past him.

"Fuck!" I curse as blue flashing lights appear in my mirrors. Cops are the last thing I need. Can't a guy catch a fucking break? They flash at me to pull over.

I take a sharp right turn down a quiet dirt path and stop, relieved to see a lone deputy in the car. Running won't help, but I have a gun stashed under the seat. It's always good to have a backup plan. I try to avoid violence, but it's not my fault if it finds me.

I lower the window as the officer approaches. He's in his mid-fifties and looks like an old-school type who might want to keep wayward kids outta jail.

"Going a little fast there, kid," he comments, tapping on the hood.

"Sorry, Officer," I reply. "Got carried away."

He squints, looking at me intently, and I stare right back.

"You're Jack's boy, aren't you?"

My jaw clenches. "What if I am?"

"You look just like him." He chuckles. "Your father wouldn't be happy if he found you out here."

My mind races through the possibilities. We're on a

quiet stretch of road. No one would know if I ran the fucker over a few times.

"Can you step out of the car, son?" he asks.

"I'm not your son," I snarl, but unclip my seat belt and get out.

He poses no risk. His holster is empty. I could take him on with bare hands if I wanted to. I'm fitter, and my mind is sharper. I chose to stay sober after seeing how alcohol and drugs fucked my mom up. Unfortunately, I still have an addiction... and it's my stepsister. Drugs or alcohol would have been better.

The officer points to the white line painted on the road and orders, "Walk along it in a straight line."

"Easy." I do as he asks perfectly. "Happy now?"

"Why don't I follow you to the house?" he suggests.

My eyebrows knot together in confusion.

"The house?" I question, trying to ascertain why he's been there before. "You know where my house is?"

"I've been visiting for years," he replies. His eyes twinkle like he's won the grand lottery prize. "Jack is an old friend. You're lucky it's me who pulled you over. Driving you back is no trouble. I'm already going to the party later."

The harmless grandpa vibes have worn off, and I see him for the twisted sonofabitch he is.

"They're good parties, right?" I keep my tone friendly and light. "Pretty girls."

The officer grins. "Like father, like son."

My fake smile twists into a snarl, and I see red.

I dive at him without hesitation and start throwing punches. I smash my fists into his smug smirk while he thrashes around like a fish gasping for air. I pin my knees on either side of his fat body to stop him from struggling. I'm not a kid anymore. Since that night with Elias, I have trained relentlessly for moments like this. Moments when I'd have to defend myself.

If he went to the parties, this sick pot-bellied fuckwit has put his shriveled cock in Clemmie, and I'd make him fucking pay for it. If he's been going for years, perhaps he fucked her before she became a woman. He's partly responsible for why she acts the way she does. He, my father, and the others are all to blame for her spreading her legs to anyone who looks in her direction.

He finally stops resisting as I knock his teeth out, and blood sprays up my arms. He's lost consciousness, but I don't stop. I punch until my chest heaves, letting the taste of iron and sweat fuel me.

I'll keep going until grandpa cop draws his last pathetic breath. I'll make sure his filthy hands never touch my Clemmie again. I want to take them all out. Every guy who has hurt her deserves to die. When his heart stops, I come out of my trance and stand, resembling a figure from a slasher movie.

I threatened Clemmie and told her I'd leave town, but I couldn't leave her at the hands of monsters.

Before returning to the mansion, I have to decide what to do with the corpse. I can't keep her safe from behind the bars of a jail cell. My attack didn't last more than five minutes, and I'm buzzing from the release of pure unadulterated rage. Adrenaline gives me the extra strength to open the trunk and haul the body inside.

It's about time I bought a new truck, anyway.

Peacefulness sweeps over me as I get into the car, happy that I've taken out another piece of trash. Apart from blood stains on the side of the road, nothing will be left of him soon enough. One of the perks of working in the garage is being responsible for taking cars to the crusher. No one would question me showing up with a vehicle to dispose of tomorrow morning, but right now, I had to get back before the party started. Clemmie may not be ready to leave yet, but I'll watch over her and wait.

Clemmie is the only reason I haven't killed Dad already. For whatever twisted reason, she loves him. But as soon as she gives me the green light, I'll remove him from the equation. I only have to worry about whether she loves him more than me.

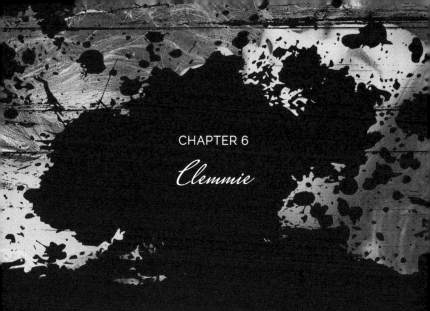

CHAPTER 6

Clemmie

"Clemmie?" Daddy knocks on my bedroom door and opens it without waiting for an answer. "Are you ready?"

"Ta-dah!" I declare, spinning around like a princess. "What do you think?"

I'm wearing a dress that was a gift from one of his friends. It's emerald green with a tight-fitting bodice. The skirt is made from thin floaty fabric with slits up the sides, making me feel like a cross between Ariel and an Egyptian goddess. The man who bought it for me likes to purchase expensive things. He's a local cop—married with a wife and kids. I don't mind him fucking me. He has to thumb in his tiny marshmallow chub, and he comes in seconds. When he's not busy with me, he likes being fucked in the ass by Daddy's special machines.

"You look beautiful." Daddy beams. His whole face lights up when he smiles, and his approval makes my insides glow. "Are you excited for tonight? We'll go down together."

"Of course, Daddy."

He holds his hand out, and I take it. We make our way to the basement. It's not a dingy place that stores old boxes; it looks like an underground nightclub. Not that I know what a real nightclub looks like, but I've seen them in movies. It has pretty flashing lights, comfortable beds, swings, ropes, and all sorts of games. Our guest list is exclusive, never more than ten people at a time. Sometimes guests bring extra girls and boys to swap and share, but I'm the only regular... and their favorite. Daddy says I should be proud that I'm the one they're fighting over to fuck.

"You're not going to disappoint Daddy, are you?" he purrs in my ear, sending goosebumps dancing over the back of my neck and down my spine. "You better be a good girl tonight, Clementine."

"I will, Daddy," I reply. "I know exactly what I have to do."

As we enter, I see a few guests have already arrived. They like to drink first. Daddy has a special machine. It looks like a robot and can make you anything you want. After the drinks are flowing, it doesn't take long for the real party to start.

Jimbo, a regular, greets Daddy as I sit on a nearby swing. I start to play, pushing my legs out in front of me. I make a 'weeee' noise as the air rushes past my face. My dress settles between my thighs and highlights the curves of my legs, but I'm still close enough to hear what the others are saying.

"Chuck's missing," Jimbo says. His wrinkles deepen like something's bothering him. "He hasn't come back from his patrol."

"We don't use real names here. You should know that by now," Daddy snaps. He doesn't like it when people talk about the outside world. That's not the point of this place.

This is a rabbit hole for you to escape into. Instead of running into the Mad Hatter or the Queen of Hearts, you're met with whips, chains, and vibrators. This is Orgasmland, not Wonderland. "Do you want your membership revoked?"

Jimbo's cheeks flush, and he stammers, "N-n-no. I didn't mean—"

"Good," Daddy says coldly. "That's the last we'll say on the subject. This is a party, after all."

The rest of the guests file in as I continue to swing. Their eyes burn into me. I like knowing they're watching, but tonight *feels* different. Although my body responds automatically to their stares, all I can think of is August and his car pulling away, leaving an emptiness inside me. We've been drawn to each other from the moment we met. I'm starting to question whether I've made the right decision to stay for the first time. Something I've never doubted before.

"My sweet peach." A man approaches to distract me from the silly thoughts in my head. He's wearing a masquerade-style mask like all the other guests. I'm wearing one too. "I thought you could help our new friends get comfortable."

Behind him, he's brought two extras. First, a young guy who looks a few years older than me. I don't like his confidence. He's checking out Daddy, and his ass cheeks are practically twitching. Next to him is a young girl. She looks around thirteen, and she's biting her lip to stop it from trembling.

"Of course," I reply brightly. Daddy has taught me to be a hostess with good manners. "Why don't I show them where we play?"

I leap off the swing, and the girl's mouth falls open. She's clearly new to this scene. If she wants to be any good or good enough for him to keep her around, she needs to up her game. I slip my hand through hers.

The young guy dismisses my help with a shake of his head. "I think I'll be fine getting acquainted," he says. "I'll speak to the others."

I resist the urge to roll my eyes as he heads toward Daddy. Daddy won't pay him any attention. He never plays at parties. That's not his job. He likes to make sure everything runs smoothly.

"You need to try and have fun," I say to the girl as I walk with her through the room. We stroll past different beds and instruments. Daddy's finest work surrounds us. It's a museum of his creative genius. "There's so much fun to be had here if you know where to look."

I lead her to a pink bed. It's the most comfortable and reserved purely for solo play. If you're on here, no one else can join you. If anyone breaks the rule, Daddy will throw them out.

"If you stay on this bed," I tell her, "no one can touch you."

Her eyes widen. "Really?"

"But you have to give them a good show," I insist. "There are so many toys here. You need to enjoy yourself to keep them interested."

"Thanks," she whispers. "I'm Crystal, by the way."

"I'm Clementine," I say, giggling and feeling some comradery. The other girls that came along never liked me. Who can blame them when their daddies want to fuck me instead of them? "Let's be best friends."

She looks at me funny, like I've misread the signals, then smiles shyly. Without August around, I need more friends. Even if I never saw this girl again, knowing I have a friend in the room makes me feel warm. I've never needed anything more than my toys before, but since August came into my life, my mind has been wired differently. He's made me enjoy the company.

"Okay," she agrees, then catches my wrist as I turn to leave. "Where are you going?"

"This is my home!" I declare, throwing my arms in the air like I'm in the middle of a grand performance. "I have to make sure our guests are happy."

Crystal lies down and makes herself comfortable as two guests come over to watch. This is the best place for her tonight.

Sometimes I try to talk with Daddy's friends, but I don't feel like entertaining them tonight. I head straight for the black leather bench. I stand and bend over it at the waist. It doesn't take long until there are a few takers. Daddy is first in line.

"Stretch your arms out," Daddy orders.

I do as he asks. He slips my wrists through restraints and locks them in place. I can be released using a combination code that only he knows.

"I may have a special surprise for you later," Daddy says as he ties a blindfold over my mask. That's part of the fun with this game.

Another pair of hands are on my ankles. They are soft hands, not like August's. They are the hands of someone more suited to working behind a desk than fixing a broken car. The men who come here are powerful and filthy rich. Daddy doesn't run his parties for free. Some attendees are tech moguls, and others are attorneys or doctors, leaving their real identities behind when they come here.

"Do it tightly," I urge, licking my lips.

The mysterious hands fasten straps around my ankles.

They're attached to a bar on the bench that will stop me from moving and keep my legs spread apart.

Soft jazz starts to play in the background. It's my favorite.

Another pair of hands push the material of my dress above my ass to get a better view. I wiggle my hips a little, knowing they'll like it.

There are grunts and whispers around me; a slippery hand eagerly reaches to paw my pussy. I respond instantly, just as I have been trained. He doesn't rub or stroke. He jabs his finger into me a few times before he removes it, and a belt buckle jingles.

A few seconds later, a small dick rudely mashes around my entrance, struggling to find the hole, then rams himself inside. It lasts less than a minute, but I moan all the same. It's what they want to hear. He should have taken Daddy's special pills. He won't impress many girls with stamina like that.

When he pulls out, another man is ready to take his place. This one isn't interested in fucking me right away. Instead of going straight for the kill, his mask tickles my ass cheeks as he spits onto my pussy. I know straight away who it is. I don't know his real name, just like I don't know any of the others, but he's gentle. He cares about making sure I'm comfortable. I like being fucked any which way, so it makes no difference to me, but making each time sensual gets him off. He's just another toy for me to play with. A cock to pass the boredom.

My hips jerk when he starts fucking me. His hands grasp my hips, and my body thuds against the bench. An orgasm builds inside me, and I can't control it as I cry out. My pussy tightening gives him the encouragement he needs as he wails. He sounds like a howling cat when he comes.

I wait for the next one after he pulls out. Usually, there'd be a queue forming, but no one is there to step up. I pout. The new girl can't be making that much of a splash, can she? Poor Crystal looks like she hasn't heard of a butt plug before, but appearances can be deceiving. Just look at me.

"Now you've had the warm-up; it's time for your special surprise!" Daddy's voice booms as something is wheeled toward me. "I have something new to trial tonight. Something many of you may want to buy and take home."

The audience claps. Daddy once said he was a magician, and I was his magical assistant. This is part of the show. A show I've been trained to be part of for years.

"Will you do the honors?" Daddy asks someone else.

Moments later, warm lube slides down my ass crack. It drips down onto my pussy, and hands smear it over my lips until they're sticky.

"Perfect," Daddy admires. He spanks my ass, making me yelp. There's a chorus of snickers as my skin wobbles. "Who wants to see what this machine can do?"

"Let's wreck her cunt," someone says.

"I want to see her pussy fucked!"

I ball my hands into fists and brace myself. I'm thankful Daddy can't see that my eyes are squeezed shut. Daddy doesn't mean to hurt me. No, he wants me to feel pleasure more than any other girl in the world, so he gives me all these special presents. He does it because he cares.

A whirring noise takes me off guard as icy steel pushes against the backs of my thighs. Whatever the machine is, it's a similar height to the bench.

"Ready?" Daddy asks the crowd.

A warm silicone dildo slides between my parted lips. It's bigger than the cock I've just taken and stings as it pushes inside me, but the initial discomfort vanishes as it slides deeper. It's ribbed with patterns, and the whole thing vibrates in different places. A ripple effect at its head spreads further down the shaft like waves.

"Who wants to control the speed?" Daddy asks.

There's a flurry of enthusiasm and volunteers. There seem to be two modes: one for the speed it fucks me and the other for vibration. Gradually the speed increases and my pussy clenches as it rubs my G-spot, teasing me closer to another orgasm. My knees are trembling, but the cuffs around my ankles keep me in place.

The machine doesn't slow down. Its vibrations intensify, putting so much pressure on my G-spot that my pussy wants to explode. The dildo starts rotating, driving me even more crazy.

"Do you want more, princess?" someone asks.

"Yes," I moan. My whole body is shaking. "More, please!"

"Make the bitch beg," another says.

They all love it, and so do I.

"Please!" I beg as the dildo withdraws with a wet pop. Lube runs down my thighs, leaving my pussy pulsing and hungry. I'd squirt if they kept going. "Please! Don't stop!"

"The little whore loves it," one purrs.

"Look at how wet she is."

"I think she needs more lubrication," Daddy says.

Men take turns spitting on my pussy and asshole. Their fluids create a sticky substance, but I can only think of Daddy's special toy and how much I want it to take me again.

The audience is getting impatient, and the dildo slides inside me again with a squelch. As well as twirling and pulsing, the head of it seems to enlarge and put additional pressure on the soft pad inside me. The pleasure is too much, and I scream as an orgasm makes my entire body quake. As I'm riding the high, the dildo detracts all the way, and my pussy makes a popping noise as liquid, spit, and lube explodes from me like uncorked champagne.

"Why don't we fuck her ass with it, too?" someone suggests.

My pussy is used to being fucked, but my ass... not after last time...

"Daddy," I gasp. He knows what happened last time. He won't let them do it again. He promised that he'd never let it happen. "Please."

"See?" A guy drawls. "She's asking nicely. Let's see it fuck her in both holes at the same time."

I can't see what's happening behind me, but I hear buzzing as Daddy adjusts his device. When the machine approaches again, it seems to have rotated. A rabbit-style vibrator comes from underneath and slides into my pussy, the ears in the perfect position to stroke my clit. This dildo doesn't fill me in the same way the other one did, but the other side that just fucked me is now heading for my ass like a missile.

"Daddy..." My voice breaks, a pitch higher. He'll know it's making me uncomfortable. "Daddy, please—"

Daddy grabs my hair roughly and yanks my head up.

"You're going to take whatever Daddy gives you."

I wince as the device aggressively stretches my asshole. It's not as big as other toys I've been made to take in the past, but it still hurts. I resist fighting it. I think of August and his hand against my panties. His hungry gaze looked like he wanted to swallow me whole. I imagine he's buried inside me as a guest cums in my hair. I spent ages conditioning it—why did they have to do that? I don't let my annoyance show. I try to relax and moan, just like Daddy wants.

"Our little anal slut enjoys getting both her holes fucked," someone says.

"Look at her filthy cunt. It's so fucking wet," another agrees. "The slut loves it."

More cum sprays over my back and ass, ruining my new dress. There's nothing I can do but take it. I'm stuck here.

Although the initial soreness has eased and my body is starting to respond to the sensations, my mind is distant. The pain that usually builds into an orgasm feels like I'm getting torn wide open. Tears sting my eyes.

What would August think if he saw me like this?

I squeeze my eyes shut and return to the pool house and how good August made me feel. He's my happy place.

CHAPTER 7

August

I swallow the acidic vomit rising in my throat as I watch through the peephole.

After washing the cop's blood away, my murderous mood hasn't disappeared. I may have stopped one man from fucking Clemmie tonight, but it hasn't stopped a line of them taking turns with her.

Clemmie isn't the only one being abused tonight. I avoid looking at the girl writhing around for a man old enough to be her father and the young man who is busy shoving his cock down a retiree's throat. I keep my eyes focused on Clemmie.

Of course, she can't see me.

I can't think straight as I watch and feel disgusted with myself for getting a raging boner. Her perfect pink pussy is so shiny and wet. I see how much she craves an orgasm from the way her back arches and the soft cry that escapes her lips as she begs the monsters to give her what she wants. I fucking hate them for reducing her to this, and it makes my heart ache.

They stop, and a machine is brought out. The only

good thing about my father's demonstration is that none of their hands are touching her precious body. Her body that they're using like it's nothing.

How did my father convince her that she enjoyed this?

I know she doesn't feel a connection to them like she does for me. She can't be attracted to them, but her pussy is dripping. She can come on demand. A skill like that doesn't come naturally. It's something *he* has trained her to do.

Did she want to make herself come when she was with me? Was her rubbing herself against my hand something she wanted and enjoyed or something her body needed to function?

My father smirks smugly, taking delight in having control. He directs the robot cock to pound into her hard. Her petite body jolts as she moans. Does she really want it? How can she even know what she wants after the life she's had?

I don't know how many hours Dad has spent exploiting her. Sometimes I question whether he killed his wife just to get Clemmie all to himself. Nothing would surprise me with him. I want to turn his face into a bloody pulp and smash him out of existence, just like the corpse in the trunk of my car. It can rot in there until tomorrow. I had to come back inside to watch over Clemmie. I had no choice.

Then, something is wrong.

I sense it instantly.

No one else does. They are leering at her like she's an animal in a zoo. She's nothing but a spectacle to devour and dispose of.

"Daddy, I..." This is the first time I've seen Clemmie hesitate or object. This is a place with no limits, but her voice wavers. "I'm..."

Her tone is pleading, desperate. She is no longer the

horny sex-loving maniac, but she sounds scared and fragile. Father's face contorts with rage. She's embarrassing him in front of the guests, and he'll make sure she pays for it later.

After fucking her ass raw, he orders the guests to get in line. He'll let them fuck her one by one. They get to choose which hole. Clemmie is a walking sex toy. A breathing doll, just like the rest of his gadgets.

Clemmie isn't moaning now. As their primal instincts kick in, the others sense her shift, making them want to fuck her harder. I can't watch this anymore. I can't stand by and let this happen.

The other parties have been different. Clemmie has always been in control of what she's doing. She seemed to enjoy it, however misguided, but this is different. I can't let it happen. Dad is punishing her for questioning him, and judging by the tent in his pants, her degradation is turning him on.

My anger reaches boiling point.

I storm through to the basement entrance, where a guard is blocking the door.

He looks up from a clipboard. "Name?"

"This is my fucking house!" I blast, trying to shoulder past him. The guard is three times my size. "Let me through!"

He blocks my path. "You're not on the list."

"I don't give a fuck if I'm not on your stupid list!" I spit. "Move out of my fucking way."

He pulls a gun out of his back pocket and presses the barrel into my forehead.

"Your father gave me strict instructions," he snarls. "It doesn't matter who you are. Shoot first, questions later."

He wouldn't be stupid enough to pull the trigger on the host's son, right? Clemmie needs my help. I want to tell her everything is going to be okay. Maybe now she'll finally understand what I've been trying to say to her for months and leave with me the next time I ask.

THWACK!

The butt of the gun rams into the side of my head.

"You fucker!" I stagger on my feet.

My thoughts are filled with images of Clemmie bent over and needing to be saved, but everything is swimming.

My knees hit the floor, and everything goes black.

CHAPTER 8

Clemmie

I HOLD A TOWEL-WRAPPED BAG OF FROZEN vegetables between my legs and sigh in relief. That'll help the swelling go down fast. My body aches like I've been hit by a train.

Daddy sits on the edge of my bed and watches me eat the special breakfast he prepared. Pancakes and maple syrup. My favorite.

"You know the rules, Clementine," Daddy says. "If you behaved, things would have turned out differently."

The sweet flavor turns bitter on my tongue.

"I'm sorry, Daddy," I say, putting down my cutlery. My stomach is in knots over disappointing him, and I don't have much of an appetite. "It won't happen again."

It's my fault they were rough with me. I shouldn't have objected. I know better than that. It's not what I've been taught to do.

"That's what I like to hear," Daddy says. "You know I hate it when you're hurting. You're my special girl, Clementine."

"I'll try to be better, Daddy," I promise.

"Good girl, I know you will," he purrs. "Now eat your pancakes."

Even after letting him down, he still made my favorite treat. I start cutting the pancakes into small pieces as he stands and claps his hands. "I have a business meeting in the city, so I'll be away until evening, but I'll see you when I get home."

"Okay," I reply. "Have a good day, Daddy."

It's not unusual for him to leave me alone for long periods. I hoped he'd take me with him when I was younger, but he never did. Now I'm happier to be left behind. I have my own means of entertainment that I can't get anywhere else.

Daddy's lips brush against my forehead in farewell. He tucks Mr. Darcey into the blankets next to me. "He can keep you company while I'm gone. Don't miss me too much."

Daddy leaves and clicks the door. Some people find silence eerie, but I like it. As soon as I finish my pancakes, I hobble to the window seat and watch Daddy's sports car disappear. I look at the empty spot where August used to park his car. He might be in the city too. Where else would he have gone? He wouldn't have returned to the town where he grew up. He hated it there.

Floorboards creak outside my door and make me jump.

"Hello?" I call.

We have a cleaner who visits weekly, but this isn't her scheduled day. The cleaner has never spoken to me before. She's discreet and doesn't ask questions. We have a gardener too, but he's never set foot inside the house, and I'm never allowed outside when he's around.

Has someone been watching the house? Do they know Daddy has gone? We have security systems, but some people are clever enough to crack them. The door handle turns, and I grab a lamp, ready to defend myself if I have to.

"August?" My mouth falls open as I see him in the doorway, and I drop the lamp. A dark bruise surrounds his left eye, and his knuckles are cut. My initial joy turns into a sulk fast. I cross my arms and pout. "I thought you left."

"I came back," he says. He looks me over, then glances at the frozen vegetables on the bed. "I saw what happened last night. I came to check that you're okay."

"The only thing I remember about my mom was her singing. Have I told you that before? She had a beautiful voice, August. She sounded like an angel. She used to sing me nursery rhymes." I change the subject to cut him off. Walking still hurts, but I lock the pain away in a box in the back of my mind. Seeing him makes me feel better. "Which one was your favorite?"

"Favorite nursery rhyme?" August frowns. "Clemmie, I'm talking about—"

"Ring-a-round the Rosie," I start singing the rhyme. "A pocket full of posies. Ashes! Ashes! We all fall down... Do you like that one, August?" I slip into my sandals. "Do you want to go for a walk in the walled garden?"

He clears his throat. "Don't you want to change?"

"No," I snap. It's a beautiful day, and my silky slip falls under my ass. I want my legs to feel the sun's warmth. "Why should I? No one else is here."

I try to walk normally, but my stance falls wider.

"You're hurt," August observes.

I start to skip to prove him wrong. He'll only use it as an excuse to hate Daddy even more. My desire not to cause problems supersedes my pain. I skip along the corridor and down the stairs, stroking the stair railings as I sing *Ring Around the Rosie* at the top of my lungs.

"Clemmie," August calls, dragging his feet behind me. "We can stay inside."

"No, we're going to the walled garden!" I insist. I spin and flash a dazzling smile. "It'll be wonderful. This way!"

He doesn't look convinced but follows me out of the house anyway. The land around the mansion spans miles. The gardener tends to the walled garden and driveway, but the rest of the grounds are wild overgrown forests. I believed fairies lived there when I was a child. I spent hours running through the trees, thinking I saw fluttering wings. I don't need to believe in fairies anymore. I have August instead.

We cross the driveway to the walled garden, and I push the gate open to reveal perfectly maintained rows of beautiful flowers. Roses, chrysanthemums, lilies... there are flowers of every color you can think of. Green leaves creep up the wall, suspending us in a place that feels far away from the mansion. The air is different here, less tense.

August continues to ask questions, but I ignore him. His voice washes over me as I focus on the chatter of birds and rustling leaves. I squeeze my eyes shut and hum, soaking in the atmosphere and appreciating how the hot rays warm my skin.

"Clemmie!" August grabs my shoulders and shakes me. "This isn't some fucking fairytale world! You were hurt last night!"

Why does he keep wanting me to relive the past?

My mouth twists into a sneer, angry that he's ruined this moment. It's a beautiful day. It should be special. What did he have to gain by going over what happened? It's none of his business.

"It looks like you were hurt too," I snarl, pointing at his face. "What happened to you?"

He buries his hands in his pockets and shifts from one foot to the other. "We're not talking about me."

I stride up to him and jab my finger into his chest. "See? Not everyone wants to talk!"

"You want to know what happened?" He towers over me. The face of my caring brother transforms into a monster consumed by fury. Something I've seen in Daddy when he gets mad. "This!" He points at his eye. "Was done by *Daddy's* security when I was coming to help you and these!" He shows me his split and bruised knuckles. "These are from stopping another fucker from hurting you!"

My bottom lip quivers. "You hurt one of Daddy's guests?"

"Don't worry, it won't get back to him that it was me." August spits on the ground. "Forget I said anything."

"Follow me," I say in a clipped tone, marching down the path.

"Clemmie?" August calls as I leave the walled garden. "Where the fuck are you going now?"

I don't stop walking. I continue into the woods by the side of the mansion, not caring that branches are catching my clothes and scratching my arms. Daddy has installed security cameras around the walled garden. Although they are not aimed at where we stand, he will see us go in and out. For a conversation like this, I need to be sure we are alone.

"Are you sure we're not gonna get lost?" August asks.

I hum and skip through the dense forest. I know the woods like the back of my hand. We don't speak for another ten minutes until we reach a stream and my favorite tree.

I stop to face him.

"What did you do to Daddy's guest, August?" I question.

His gray-eyed stare burns into mine, and he replies, "I killed him."

My heart jolts, not from disgust but from curiosity.

"May I?" I nod at his hands. He shrugs but doesn't push me away as I take them in mine and trace my fingers over his cuts. They really are something. My voice is breathier than usual as I ask, "How did it feel?"

"It wasn't enough, Clem!" August snatches his hands away, making my chest ache. Why does he like hurting me? "Killing him didn't change anything. You still got hurt last night. *He* let those animals do awful things to you. I would kill them all if I could, and I would have tried if the guard didn't knock me out."

"Do you want to know a secret, August?" I take his hands again. They are double the size of mine, and he winces as I stroke the splits in his skin. They are marks of his love. Marks that show how much he cares. He threatened to leave me, but he wouldn't. He could never go now that I know this about him. I step closer, so close our bodies are almost touching, and whisper, "Sometimes I want to hurt people too."

"But you wouldn't hurt his guests, would you?" August sneers, tearing his hands out of my grasp. He doesn't wait for me to answer because he knows he's right. "After what they did to you last night, don't you want to punish them? Dad treats you as a prop. You're just another toy to display for his twisted friends at his show. It's sick!"

Hot tears spill down my cheeks.

"You're wrong!" I shout, making birds in a nearby tree fly away.

"You don't hurt people you love, Clemmie," August says gently. "What he's done to you is wrong. He doesn't love you, not how you think he does."

"You're messing with my head, August," I say. "You want to get between us and tear us apart. This is what Daddy warned me about. He said someone like you would try to take me away from him. I'm special. He says I'm special, okay?"

"Clemmie..." His voice softens as he strokes my cheek. He looks at me the same way you'd look at a puppy about to be put down. "Of course you're special. You're perfect, but real love isn't about hurting the people you love."

"What do you know about love, August?" I turn vicious. "No one has ever loved you the way Daddy loves me. Maybe if your mom loved you more, you wouldn't be—"

I don't get to finish my sentence. August grabs my throat and slams me backward into a tree. I yelp as his face gets close to mine; his hot breath tickles my cheeks.

"Don't talk about her like that. You don't know anything, Clemmie. You think you know everything, but you're nothing but Dad's dirty secret," August snarls. "Do you think he'll want you when you're older? Do you think any of his guests will want you then? There will be someone new. Someone younger. Someone will take your place. You're not his real daughter."

He drops his hold, and I fall to my knees, holding my neck and gasping for air.

I don't have the strength to get up again. Sobs overcome my body, and I pull my knees to my chest.

Maybe August is right.

CHAPTER 9

August

I SNAPPED.

I shouldn't have, but I did, and now she's rocking back and forth in the dirt like I've crushed her fucking soul. Fuck! I tried to be nice. I wanted to show I was willing to do anything for her, but none of that made a difference. It's never enough. *I* am never enough.

Maybe Clemmie was right about Mom too. I never felt loved by her. I was nothing but an inconvenience. An extra mouth to feed that she never wanted. I've never felt love like I have for Clemmie. Our relationship is fucked up, and she's my addiction, but I'll never leave her.

"Clemmie, I should never have said it like that," I duck and put my hand on her shoulder. "I'm trying to look out for you."

She sniffs and looks up. Her green irises stand out against her bloodshot eyes, and they narrow at me. "You're right. You shouldn't have said it at all."

"I only said it because I care... because I love you... because I want you to know what real fucking love feels like and to see him for who he really is."

"You don't love me!" Clemmie snarls, wiping her tears away. "If you did, you'd show me how you felt. All you do is threaten to leave, tell me how much you hate Daddy, and run away whenever I show you affection. Those men may have hurt me last night, but at least they wanted me. You don't want me, August!"

"Clem..." I struggle to find the right words. "Of course I want you. It's just—"

"It's just, what?" Her eyes blaze with anger. "You get jealous when you see me with other men. You kill other men to stop them from hurting me, but you don't want to be with me. You want me to run away with you, but you can't bear to touch me. You make no sense!"

"I don't want to be like them!" I blast. "You mean more to me than anyone else, and that's why I don't want to treat you like they do, but it doesn't mean I don't want you."

She crosses her arms over her chest.

"Prove it," she demands.

This is a moment which there is no going back from.

I can either run like I always do or give her what she desires and what I've been unable to stop thinking about since I laid eyes on her. Clemmie doesn't believe I care, but if I show her how much I do, I'd never want her to touch another man again. I want her to belong to me.

I grab her waist and pull her toward me. I've spent so long pushing her away that feeling her tiny body and her silky nightgown against my skin feels right. Her sweet shampoo fills my nostrils, and something else too. *Her scent.* The smell of home.

This isn't the pool house at midnight. We're in the woods, surrounded by trees, and there's no one else around. If I didn't know better, this could be from a fairytale. I wish it were. I wish this place were far away from here. A safe place where it was only the two of us, and the real world couldn't touch us.

I've spent months denying our connection because I've wanted to play the role of her brother and haven't wanted to share her with my father. I've ignored what matters most and what my heart has been telling me. I want Clemmie to be mine and mine alone.

Her chin tips up, and the sun hits her hair, illuminating her in a golden glow. Her lips part as she goes to kiss me, and I don't back away. Our lips brush, then we kiss. Our mouths and tongues explore each other hungrily like we're the air the other needs to breathe. Her small fists grab and cling onto my T-shirt as if I'm the very thing anchoring her to this godforsaken world, and I hold her so fucking tight because I'm afraid of what'll happen if I let go.

All of my worries disappear. Everything else is irrelevant when she's in my arms and her lips are on mine. We came into this world on the same day and were set on a fucked-up path, but now we've found each other, I never want to let her go. I couldn't protect Mom, but I wasn't going to let history repeat itself.

We kiss until her lips are red and puffy, but I catch her hand as it slides down my chest and rests on my erection. I almost cum in my pants at her touch, but I don't. Succumbing to my desires should feel wrong, but I've never felt so right or complete.

"What's wrong?" Clemmie asks, her expression turning fearful. "Don't you like it?"

I put my thumb to her lips to silence her.

"Of course, I do," I growl, wanting nothing more than for her to wrap her thighs around me and fuck her until she cries my name. "But you're hurt. I'm not gonna hurt you some more."

"Please, August," she pleads. Her eyelids are hooded with lust. "I need more. I need to feel all of you. I really fucking need you."

She has me at the word 'need.'

"Lie down," I instruct. "I want to show you there is more to making love than machines and groups of strangers. I'll show you the real difference between fucking and making love."

She does as I ask. The mossy ground is surprisingly soft, softer than other mattresses I've slept on in the past. Clemmie's hair splays around her head like a blonde halo. Her silky lilac slip shows off her pointed nipples and dips between her thighs, where I know she'll be wet and waiting for me. But I don't want to hurt her. I'm gonna make this last. I'll show her how much she means to me and prove there's so much more to sex than what she's been used to.

I roll on top and part her legs, balancing my arms on either side of her head. My hardness pushes into her stomach, and she wiggles beneath me to find a better angle. She's trying to rush it, but I won't let that happen.

"Clemmie," I say firmly, "if we're doing this, we're doing it my way."

In this world, our world, nothing else matters. All that does is the fact that we are together, finally.

I stroke a loose hair out of her eyes and stare into them. Her pupils dilate, and her cheeks flush with delight. I lean forward, my face hovering less than an inch away from hers. Our lips are so close that I can feel static in the air between us, but I don't kiss her again... not yet.

"August," she breathes, rolling her hips. "Please. I need you."

My heart hammers against my ribs. Her lithe body at my mercy makes it impossible to pull away, even if I wanted to. I'm impressed she doesn't try to kiss me again. She holds herself back, and her inner thighs clench as she battles to resist her urges. She's trying to do this my way, and it makes her even hotter.

This is the point of no return.

I reward her for her patience and kiss her hard and deep. I consume her, breathing in her scent, flowers, musk, and safety. She moans into my mouth. Our kiss is filled with longing, secrets, and sadness at all the wasted nights sleeping under the same roof and never getting this close. She catches my lip between her teeth and nibbles it, teasing a growl from the back of my throat.

I have to be careful and remind myself not to lose control, despite the primal urges she draws out of me. I can't flip her over and fuck her until she's drained me of every last drop of cum. No, I have to take it slow.

I'm overcome with the need to taste her. The overwhelming need to devour every little piece of her. I slide down her body, slipping the straps off her shoulders and kissing along her collarbone. She wriggles in approval as I continue my exploration, something I've been dreaming about for the longest time. I run my hands over her slip, admiring the delicate curves of her body and their contrast with her sharp ribs. As soon as I get her away from here, I'll make sure she eats proper food. Father likes keeping her tiny because it makes her look younger.

"August," Clemmie moans. "I need... more... I need you."

"We're doing this my way," I remind her.

I pull the neck of her slip down, exposing her milky breast with a pointed, pink nipple begging to be sucked. The same tits I've been wanking over since I first saw her topless. I knead her skin, then pinch her nipple between my thumb and forefinger, making her buck.

Shit. They're even more perfect up close.

I take her nipple in my mouth. My tongue flicks over the peak as she moans in pleasure. I suck it while kneading and massaging the skin around it, then use my other hand to play with her other nipple.

"August!" Clemmie's back arches as I work on her. Her hips gyrate and push against me. As they do, wet fabric rubs against me. Her breathing grows short and ragged. I can smell her arousal from here, but I'm not done with her perfect little tits yet.

Clemmie is used to sex being used as an exchange. Her body has been used to trial Dad's new creations or for making an old guy come to further a business venture, but I'm making this experience all about her. I've never had any complaints from women I've slept with in the past, but none of them have responded to me like Clemmie.

She claws at my back, making my cock even harder. Her scratches make me want to prolong my teasing. I sink my teeth into her tit to warn her not to rush me before returning to lapping and playing with her nipples. She throws her head back and moans. It takes me a few seconds to realize she's coming. I didn't know that was a thing, but fuck. I'd suck her tits for hours if the thought of her wet pussy wasn't so damn hard to resist.

"I'm just getting started," I say.

"August!" She grabs my hair. "It's... so..."

"Do you want me to stop?" I ask, scared I've done something wrong.

"No!" she growls, making me chuckle.

"Good," I purr, slipping down her body. "Now let me take care of you."

Clemmie spreads her legs wide as I go down further. Soaked fabric nestles between her thighs. It's the only barrier stopping us from crossing a line that I know we shouldn't, but...

I stop myself from diving face-first into her pussy and keep going. I stop at her ankles, looking at the blue bruises that have formed from where she was restrained. My stomach churns at the memory, but I shower them with kisses and continue up her legs. I slide up the silky fabric as she rests her feet on my back, and I stroke behind her knees.

"That tickles!" Her laugh is gleeful, but I notice her lust-filled gaze as I look up. I grasp her hips to yank her forward and bite her inner thigh. She cries out, then my fingers trace over her delicate skin and kiss the spot better. I wanted to leave my mark on her. Claim her. Show every other fucker that every inch of her belongs to me, and I'm not sharing.

Trees rustle above us, carrying our secret away in the breeze.

What would they say if they could talk?

Fuck. I can't hold myself back anymore.

Her panties have been sucked into her swollen slit, and I run my finger down the wet line. This is different from the last time I touched her. That time she rocked against me. This time, I'm in control.

"Does my pussy feel as good as you thought it would?" she asks. For someone who looks like an angelic fairy, she has a dirty fucking mouth, which is a huge turn-on. "Can you feel how wet I am for you, August? Can you feel how much my pussy is dripping for you?"

"You're really fucking wet," I compliment, pulling her panties down. They're the prettiest purple panties I've ever seen, but they're not as pretty as what lies beneath.

I've seen her pussy before, but never this close. Her lips are pink and a little swollen from yesterday. I know her ass will be covered in bruises, but if she's in pain, she doesn't show it. I kiss the crease at the top of her thighs and lick along it. I'm going to treat her how she deserves to be treated.

There is no going back now. After trying to leave town last night, I have to accept that there's an inevitability about us. Our growing attraction has been like watching a car crash happen in slow motion. I've been trying to regain control of the car and fight against the wheel, but it's been no good. We were heading straight for a tree, and I couldn't stop it. Now I've given up trying and accepted that if we were gonna burn, we'd burn together.

"I need you," Clemmie whines. "I need you to taste me, August. Please."

I hold her hips and lick down her slit. The flat of my tongue laps her pussy, concentrating on the pool of juices at her opening. She's sweet, but there's something else mixed in there. I don't let myself think about what happened last night and the traces a shower can't erase. I know what parts of her are her, and fuck... she's my fucking kryptonite. Her clit throbs for my attention, and I circle my tongue over it, making her sigh. I love how her body responds to me and how she squeezes her tits in response.

"August."

Her moans send a lightning bolt straight to my cock. I've seen her fuck other people, but nothing compares to hearing my name coming out of her mouth. I lightly probe her entrance with my tongue and push myself inside her, wanting to get lost and clean all those fucking demons out of her sweet little hole.

She wails as I tongue fuck her. Her thighs clench around my head, and I suck her pussy lips gently.

"August!" she cries out again, grabbing a handful of my hair.

I put my mouth over her clit to create a seal and suck another orgasm out of her. Her thighs shake as her wetness coats my chin. She's a gusher, and I lick it up, wondering how good and slippery she will feel all over my dick.

Clemmie laughs and grins when she's done, making me glance up. Her eyes sparkle with exhilaration as if we've been on a rollercoaster. "Why did you make me wait so long?"

"You know why," I reply playfully.

"I want to feel your cock inside me, August," she chirps, spreading her legs as wide as they can go as an invitation. "I want to feel every inch of you."

I hesitate. As much as I want to fuck her more than I've ever wanted anything, I don't want to hurt her.

"You'll be hurting me if you don't," she says, reading my mind, then adding, "I'm not the only one who needs this."

She's right, but I don't show it.

"It's your turn to lie down, August," she orders. "Or are you forgetting we can read each other's minds?"

I follow her instructions because my boner is digging into my pants so hard that my balls might explode if I don't release it soon. Clemmie unbuckles my belt and undoes my zipper.

"Pull them down, August," she says.

I release my cock as she asks, and her face lights up.

"There's no going back after this," I warn her.

I need to give her an out if she wants it.

She ignores my words and wastes no time straddling

me. She guides her wet pussy juice over my shaft, soaking me in her cream and my spit.

"I don't want to go backward," she breathes, positioning the tip of my cock at her entrance. She pauses, then mounts me with a loud sigh and lets me sink into her depths. "We were always meant to be together, August. You know that too; otherwise, you wouldn't have come back."

Her walls are still pulsing from her orgasms. They are squeezing and holding onto my cock like it doesn't want to let go... and I don't want her to. I never want to let her go again. I grab her ass, and she falls forward, pushing her perky tits against me as she kisses me hungrily.

"Go slow," I urge. "I want to enjoy the feel of your tight pussy. I want to make this last."

I don't need her to fuck me at jackhammer speed; I want to savor every fucking second. I've dreamed of this for months, but the reality is a million times better. Her pussy is hot, wet, and oh so fucking tight. Clemmie takes the hint. She rides me slowly, her hips circling in torturous circles, letting me get lost in the moment and how amazing she feels.

"I've been waiting for this for months, August," she whispers. "I've been dreaming about how it would feel to climb onto your cock and ride it."

Her words only drive me crazier. She scrapes her teeth along my neck and latches on.

"Clem," I groan as her ass slaps down hard, making my balls clap against her as the tip of my cock feels like it hits a wall. She doesn't move again until she's sucked on my neck hard.

"There!" She sits up triumphantly, swinging her hair over her shoulder and sending it cascading down her back.

She wipes her thumb over my neck. "Now you have my mark on you."

I growl, overcome with lust and wanting to turn her smug smirk into a breathy moan. I sit up, pulling her ass closer and pressing her tits against me. She wraps her arms around me. If anyone walked past, her slip would hide my cock and her wet juices coating my lap. I hold her ass cheeks and turn her over, so I'm lying on top of her. Her ankles rest behind my back, making her pussy clench tightly around me, and I start to fuck her hard.

I wanted to be gentle, but she's too fucking hot, and I'm too far gone.

I'm desperate. All the months I've been waiting culminate and explode in a frenzy as I rail her, making her bounce and squeal until there are no birds within a mile radius.

"I'm going to come, August," she says, "I'm going to come all over your fucking cock, and I want you to fill me. Fill me right up until I can't take any more."

My balls tighten, wanting to spray her insides, but I keep going until she's screaming my name. Her hips buck wildly as her pussy spasms around me. This isn't the same as how she fucks other people. She's coming undone, and it's all because of me.

"Fill me, August," Clemmie begs as she gushes, showering me with her cream. It's my turn next. "Fuck!" She writhes as my cock teases every drop of her orgasm from her. "I love you, August."

"Fuck!" I grunt as I let go and release.

I lock my eyes on hers as I come. She thrusts her hips upward, making sure my thick cum is filling her, and she won't miss a drop. It's the best fucking orgasm of my life, and I've filled her with more than cum. I've claimed her as mine, and I won't be sharing her. I can't.

I roll off her with a sigh and stare at the blue sky above us, still thinking about what she said. She loves me, but does she love me the same way I love her? Like I am willing to throw down my whole life to make her happy?

I turn my head to look at her next to me, still panting. My eyes sweep over her body. A body I've been inside. She pulls her slip down, hiding my sticky cum that's defiled her pussy which is now red and raw.

"Hey," I say, pulling her close. Her body fits perfectly under my arm, and I inhale her scent. "Come here."

Neither of us speaks. For someone who talks a lot, I've never known Clemmie to be this quiet.

"Clemmie?" I ask eventually, breaking the silence. "Are you okay? I didn't hurt you, did I?"

"No," she says, then grins wickedly, "but I'd like to do that every day, August."

I smile and kiss her nose. A few freckles under her eyes come out in the summer, and I see them now.

"Then we can," I say. "If you leave this place with me."

"You didn't say it back," she mutters.

It takes a second to realize what she's talking about.

"I didn't say it back because I didn't think I had to," I say. "You know how I feel about you, Clemmie."

"Then say it."

"I love you," I murmur, stroking her shoulder as she clings to me. "That's why I want you to leave with me."

"It's not that easy," she says. Her body stiffens. "It's okay here. It's safe in this house, but it's not safe for people like me out there."

"People like you?" Dad's done a fucking number on her if she thinks she's the one in the wrong. She doesn't understand that she's the victim. "There's nothing wrong with you."

"I'm not like other people, don't you see?" Clemmie sits up abruptly. "I'm not made like other people. I do things for fun. Bad things. Bad things make me happy."

"It's because he's made you do those things!" My nostrils flare in anger. "None of it is your fault. You had no choice."

Why didn't my mom hurry up and die sooner? In a way, her death is the only good thing she's done for me. It brought me to Clemmie.

"No, you don't understand." Clemmie shakes her head. "It's who I am. It's time I show you something."

"Show me something?"

She stands up and holds out her hand for me to take. "It's time I show you my pet."

CHAPTER 10

Clemmie

"WHERE ARE WE GOING?" AUGUST ASKS.

I dance through the forest, feeling on top of the world. I want to slip off my sandals and wriggle my toes in the dirt, but I should keep them on for where we're going. I raise my hands, stroking the leaves as I pass. They're so soft, so full of life.

August finally fucked me.

I knew it was what he wanted. It's what we've both been waiting for, and it was even better than I imagined. I could see inside his head, and that's how I knew he wanted me more than anything. August said that sex is about more than fucking, and now I'm starting to understand what he means.

"How much further?" August grumbles.

He hasn't been this far onto our land before.

August thinks Daddy keeps me prisoner, but he doesn't realize Daddy has given me the ability to be free and embrace every part of myself. He has parties in the basement, but these woods are mine.

"It's not far from here," I chirp, then say to the air, "I'm coming, my darlings!"

"Huh?" I turn back to see August's eyebrows lower in confusion.

He'll see soon enough.

"Here we are!" I declare, skipping to the center of the clearing. Daddy is right about this place. It is the perfect spot. It's not until I duck to clear away all the branches and leaves that August sees what I'm doing. "Ta-dah!"

This is the door to the underneath.

Is August ready for what he's about to see?

Of course he is! I tell myself. August loves me. If he can screw someone he sees as a sister, he's ready for this. If he loves me, he'll understand, and if he doesn't... well, I have another solution for that, which I'd rather not think about.

August kneels to get a better view of the trapdoor. "What the fuck is this?"

"Daddy isn't the only one who plays with toys," I say, leaning to key in the code that keeps the door shut. "His playroom is in the house, but mine? It's here."

There's a beep, and it slides to reveal concrete steps that lead into darkness. No one else is around, but I steal a look over my shoulder to make sure we're alone. Daddy has a lot of security measures to ensure no one crosses the perimeter. Even if they did find it, they'd never get in without the code.

I head down the steps, pausing to turn on the light and illuminate the concrete in an amber glow. It reminds me of candles flickering, making it cozy.

"Come on, August." I turn to him and grin, offering him my hand. "You're safe with me, I promise."

"I'm the one who should be keeping you safe," he mutters but slides his fingers through mine.

His giant hands consume my tiny palms, just like his massive dick destroyed my pussy. He's bigger than any man I'd taken before, including Daddy. After taking every inch of his deliciousness, walking was even more painful, but the ache was nice. It's a friendly reminder of how he succumbed to his desires. A reminder of how we are meant to be.

"Jesus, Clemmie." He puts his spare arm up to cover his mouth and nose as I close the hatch behind us. "What's that smell?"

"You get used to it," I reply, leading him down the steps to the corridor.

The smell used to bother me, but it doesn't faze me now. I have a strong stomach. I've spent so long down here that the smell of human shit, blood, and piss is about as homely as the mansion. This isn't the kind of hole a serial killer digs in their garden to hide victims; this is properly constructed. It has a purpose.

"This is one of the reasons Daddy bought this place," I explain to him as we go along the long corridor. "There are tunnels that lead back to the house and his basement."

I take a few turns. It's worlds away from the forest above. I like that. Sometimes I think about how this land is like me. No one knows what's hiding underneath.

"What the fuck is down here?"

I click my tongue impatiently. August is full of questions. He needs to learn to listen more.

"I told you! I keep my pets here," I say. I drop his hand and skip ahead. My face lights up as I come to another door. "In here!"

I turn the handle to the dungeon. Here is where Daddy dumps people who don't behave. People who deserve to be punished. Daddy and I have a deal. I go to his parties, and he brings me live bodies. People who can help me live out *my* fantasies.

August pales as he looks at my pet. "What the…"

CHAPTER 11

August

A SACK OF SHIT COWERS BEFORE ME. HE'S AN older man. Older than our father, in his sixties maybe. Chains attached to the wall are shackled to his ankles and wrists to secure him. He yelps when he sees us, and his bloodshot eyes widen in fear.

"What's wrong?" Clemmie taunts, cocking her head to the side. All of her timidness vanishes. "Are you not happy to see me, little pet?"

His cheeks are sallow, and his ghostly, gray skin looks like it hasn't seen the sun in weeks.

"Please!" he gasps. Tears fall down his filthy cheeks, leaving grimy lines behind. I wrinkle my nose as I discover the source of the foul smell. A hole in the floor in the corner of the room looks to feed directly into the sewage line. The chains tying him are long enough for him to make it that far, but no further. He ignores Clemmie and looks at me. He starts pleading, "You have to help me! I have kids and a wife! They'll want to see me again."

Clemmie giggles like a guy begging for his life is as funny as a comedy show.

"Blah, blah, blah!" She mocks him and rolls her eyes. "You're lucky to still be here at all. Not like the others."

The man trembles in fear at the tiny girl threatening him. I don't recognize him from Dad's parties or from around town. After everything she's been through, I know Clemmie has issues, but there is an unhinged look on her face that I've never seen before. For so long, I thought our father was the one who fucked her up, but now I'm not so sure.

I don't know what to say or ask as I spot scraps of stale bread. "Who is he?"

How long has he been here? And, more importantly, what has she been doing to him?

"I told you, August," she drawls, "he's my pet. Daddy got him for me. If he's not careful, he'll end up like my last one." Her tone is venomous as she shoots a look of disdain in his direction, and the man omits a pathetic howl from his chapped lips. "Bad pets get put down."

I grab her arm and steer her out of the room, slamming the door behind us. I wish I could forget the scene that lay beyond it.

Who is she? I've always wanted to protect her from harm. I killed someone for her, but it doesn't seem like she needs my protection.

Clemmie pouts like we're back in the pool house, and even though we're in this rat-infested dungeon, my cock betrays me. Her lips are so fucking kissable.

"What is it?" Clemmie asks. She trails her finger up my forearm across my tense muscles, then eyes the bulge in my pants and smiles. "You said you loved me, August. I wanted to show you all of me. You wanted to understand why I don't want to leave here, so I'm showing you."

I gulp. I'm unsure whether I want to hear the answer, but I have to ask, "What are you going to do with him?"

"The same as everyone else does with their pets," she says like it's obvious. "I'll play with him until I get bored."

My fists clench in anger and disbelief. "You'll fuck that?!"

Dad gets her to fuck random strangers, but they don't look like they've been sleeping in their shit for weeks.

"Is that what you think of me, August?" Her face falls. "Do you really think I'm Daddy's little whore who will fuck anything? No, of course I don't fuck him! He's my science experiment, just like those who came before him."

"How many pets have you had?"

"I'm not sure you really want to know," she says, turning away from me, "or if you can handle it."

I think back to how I killed the cop. Despite my concussion, I drove to the junkyard and watched as the crusher decimated the car with the body still inside. No one would ever find him in a block of metal.

My voice is low and gravelly, "You have no idea what I can handle."

"We'll see about that," she replies. "Follow me."

I can tell from the swing of her hips that she's testing me as she guides me further down the corridor. She wants to see how much I can take before I break. My love for her keeps me going. She's fucking insane, but she seems to have experience and know what she's doing. She has an added confidence that she doesn't have in the mansion. She adopts a persona for the parties, always keen to perform and do what he wants, but it's different here. Everything else is stripped away. This is her lair.

"Over here." She beckons me to another door that's

locked with a keypad. Father's tight-knit security measures have benefits, after all. A green flash of light, and the door clicks open. "Are you sure you're ready for this?"

Her voice is teasing, but I refuse to show fear. Her unpredictability is terrifying but mesmerizing. How can she be capable of sending a chill down my spine and blood to my cock simultaneously?

"Show me," I demand.

I take a deep breath as we step inside.

It's not what I expected. After seeing her pet and the dungeon, I'd anticipated something similar, but this is different. It's almost like a museum. The room is filled with various artifacts, and there's too much to take in at once.

An assortment of objects hanging on the walls draws my attention first. Stuffed body parts are mounted in the same way that a hunter would display a prized kill. The walls don't hold the only items of interest. A workbench takes up a large space in the middle of the room, equipped with many tools and a comfy-looking armchair. A stack of books and sewing equipment sits to the chair's right. A sewing machine rests on another smaller table to the left of that.

The longer I look at the room's contents, the more I understand. My stomach drops at the sight of a lampshade made of skin and chairs that have human feet as legs. I count the body parts and try to calculate how many pets Clemmie has kept.

What ornament would she turn me into if she had enough of me? Would my chest end up on a coffee table, or my cock be used as a handle or coat hook?

"What do you think, August?" Clemmie asks. "This is my special place."

My palms are clammy, but I hide my shock. "How many people have you killed, Clemmie?"

"That's not a question to ask a lady," she replies, her green eyes sparkling.

How can she joke around?

I try to keep my cool, but her casualness annoys me. My father isn't the only one with a twisted appetite. In some fucked up way, I can see now how they're made for each other. But where does that leave me, and what is my place in our fucked-up family?

"Where do you find them?" I ask.

"Daddy brings them to me," she says. "I don't ask questions."

"What do you do to them? Before turning them into..." I screw up my face at the sight of a cushion made from varying human hair colors. "This."

"It depends on my mood." She takes a seat in the armchair and curls her legs underneath her. "Some of them I like to keep longer than others."

"When did it start?"

She bites her lip in concentration. "It started with animals first. I was young and used to play outside near our old house. Squirrels mainly, then other small creatures who tried to ruin my fairy dens. Daddy caught me with a neighbor's cat one night, and he wanted to help. We moved out here after that. It suited both of us."

"When did you progress to people?" I ask.

Clemmie may have a predisposition to violence, but no child is born a killer. Father encouraged her behavior. He made her this way. Even now, there's no way she could overpower an adult man alone.

"I was twelve when I had my first proper kill," she says, "but it's taken years to get the technique right. Sometimes I care more about the process. Other times, it's more about what I can do afterward. I like crafting. It helps pass the time. These are my creations. Recently, that's what I've preferred more."

"Twelve?" I gawp at her. "How do you do it?"

"Oh, that's easy!" She jumps up and strolls to a cabinet, popping it open. It looks like a pharmacy counter on the inside. My mouth goes dry as I see the needles, not because I'm scared of them but because I've seen them poking out of my mom's arms for years. "I drug them."

"Does he..." I try to get my thoughts straight. "Does he help you do this?"

"He brings them to me sedated, then leaves the rest up to me," she explains and gestures at the hospital trolley beds. "I move them around on these."

I've always pitied Clemmie for being trapped in a prison of my father's making. Now I'm questioning whether the reason he's kept her locked away isn't that he wants to keep her to himself, although I'm sure that's part of it, but because he knows it's too dangerous to let her loose on the outside world.

"What do you think?" she asks, snapping me out of my reverie.

Her prior confidence evaporates as she seeks my approval with her wide beautiful eyes. The eyes of a serial killer.

I sigh and run my hands through my hair. "I don't know what to say, Clem."

"You think I'm a bad person, don't you?" She wrings her clasped hands. "You think I'm a monster too."

"Hey!" I walk over and put a finger under her chin, tipping her face up. "You could never be a monster to me."

"Do you understand why I can't leave now?" she says. "Where else am I going to be able to do this?"

I refuse to believe she's beyond saving.

He has enabled her behavior.

How would she know what she is missing if she hasn't had a chance to live an ordinary life?

"Don't you want to be able to see more of the world?" I ask. "There's more to life than keeping pets and fucking Dad's friends."

"But I don't know who I am," she whispers. "I'm in control of everything here. Daddy loves me, and so do his friends."

"Did they love you yesterday while they were watching you get hurt and shooting their loads inside your bleeding ass?"

She winces, letting her true feelings show.

"I make my pets hurt too, August," she says matter-of-factly. "Doesn't that make me as bad as them and deserving of the pain? It's only fair."

No matter what she does, I know I'll never truly think badly of her. It doesn't matter how many fucked up things she does or how many men she's killed. She's still my Clemmie.

"Fair would be giving life a chance above ground," I say, stroking her cheek. I can't keep my hands off her. I want to take her out of these godforsaken tunnels. I may not know how good life can be yet, but I want to be better for her. *For us.* "Don't you want to see what else is out there?"

She rises from the chair and takes my hand. "I've not been as interested in my pets since I met you, August. I'm different when you're around. I don't need to... you know... but out there, I don't know whether I can exist without this part of myself."

"But I'll be right there with you," I say. I don't say that I'd kill for her again, but I know I would. "If you leave with me, every day can be like today. We can start over. Would you like that?"

This usually is when she'd argue, but she whispers, "I'll think about it."

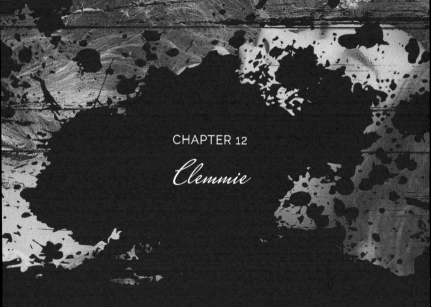

CHAPTER 12

Clemmie

My underground den is usually my favorite place to go. It's where I come to relax and unwind, but August's words echo around my head.

Did I want to try and live above ground? I've read about life outside of these walls.

I love my creations. My special room bursting with my beloved treasures is the best part about our home and the tunnels beneath it, but is August right about there being more to life than this? This is all I've ever known. Daddy has explained that people out there would never understand me. He said I don't belong anywhere but here, but Daddy also said he would never hurt me, and he did last night.

What if everything Daddy and I have is built on a lie?

August has shown me how orgasms feel even better when you like the person you're fucking, so maybe he's telling the truth about everything else too.

I let August out of the tunnels an hour ago. He'll be back in the main house already. Daddy will return soon, and I don't want him to know about August being here. This place is our little secret.

"What do you think I should do?" I ask.

My pet is no help. All he does is whimper as I stick my needle through his ear. He's slowly losing consciousness from the drugs. Crafting isn't giving me my usual buzz, and I'm clumsy. I pride myself on the care I take with my creations, but I've already dropped two stitches.

Fuck. I sit astride my pet, not bothered by the smell, and curse as the thread slips out. I lick the end of it and push it through the needle's eye. If he wakes and sees me here, he won't be able to move with his legs and arms tied down.

I'm done with his ears. I move onto his mouth and start sewing his lips closed with black thread. I enjoy the feeling of his skin popping as I pull it through. He's like a doll. My special doll who will be silent forever.

A bang from further down the tunnels startles me.

"August?" I jump off my pet's lap, leaving the needle stuck in his lip. I poke my head out of the dungeon. "August, is that you?"

"Clementine." Daddy's voice makes my blood run cold as he turns the corner.

He doesn't come here unless he's delivering a new toy to play with, and he lacks his usual upbeat tone. He is mad. Really mad.

"Daddy!" I step out and shut the door behind me. My latest craft project could be finished later. "You're home early."

"I am," he snarls. "When I found out you showed your brother our secret place, I left my meeting early."

My chest constricts like someone is squeezing the air out of my lungs.

Daddy holds up his phone, revealing camera footage of the forest and the entrance to my den. On the screen, I open the door, and August follows me. Daddy doesn't have surveillance underground for obvious reasons, but he must have installed hidden cameras without my knowing. It wouldn't have been difficult to install them in the trunk of a tree hidden from view.

"Daddy." My bottom lip trembles in fear. "I can explain."

"Come with me, Clementine," he says.

I fall into line behind him and follow.

He's wearing his favorite crisp black suit and shiny shoes that squeak as he walks. He leads me through the tunnels, along the passageway leading to the house. He presses the ring on his finger into a panel to open a hidden door to the basement. He's the only one with permission to connect the two areas.

As soon as I step into the basement, he spins and slams his hands into the wall on either side of my head, boxing me in with no escape. His gray eyes darken, a storm raging behind them. I've never seen him this furious before.

"Your brother is a problem," he hisses in a menacing tone. "I welcomed him into our home in good faith, but I never expected you would show me such disobedience. He's a bad influence on you, Clementine. Did you have anything to do with the missing cop?"

"No," I stammer, but August might.

"Don't lie to me!" Daddy roars, spraying me with spit. "It was you, wasn't it? You killed him, didn't you? Did you get him to help you?"

"No, Daddy," I whimper. "I swear, I've only hurt the pets you gave me."

"I don't believe you." Daddy's expression is thunderous. "Is that why you showed August the basement? Have you found someone to share in your twisted desires?"

"He's not like me, Daddy," I try to defend him. I saw August's expression when he saw my pet for the first time. He tried to hide it, but it shocked him. He makes out he's big and tough when I'm the one who has to be strong for both of us. "I made a mistake by showing him our special place. He never asked to see it. It was all me, I swear!"

Daddy slaps me hard across the cheek, sending my face flying to the left and almost knocking me over.

"Why did you show him?" he presses.

"I don't know," I stammer. "It just happened."

He doesn't know about August fucking me. If he did, he wouldn't be asking for answers; he'd have already started with my punishment.

"Nothing just happens!" he explodes. He steps back, and his eyes scan my body. His mouth twists into a cruel snarl as my nipples harden involuntarily under his scrutiny, but the look in Daddy's eyes tells me what's about to happen next will not be for my pleasure. "You're nothing but an attention-seeking whore. Look at you. This is not what I trained you for. You were missing attention because Daddy left town, weren't you?"

I hang my head, deciding this will be the best way to proceed, and murmur, "Yes."

He grabs a fistful of my hair roughly and forces me to meet his gaze, "Yes, what?"

"Yes, Daddy," I answer dutifully. "I'm an attention whore."

"That's right," he sneers. "And what happens to whores who crave attention?"

"We deserve to be punished."

I know what I did was wrong.

I broke Daddy's trust by taking August to my special place, but I had no other choice. I needed to show him who

I really am. If August meant what he said about us leaving together, he had to know the real me before he could make a decision. I'd take Daddy's punishment if it meant protecting the small part of me that is starting to consider a new life with August.

Daddy unbuckles his belt and takes his cock out. "You know what to do."

I get on my knees, and he pushes his cock to the back of my throat, making me gag. He thrusts until I'm choking and gasping for air.

It's just a blowjob. An act I've done hundreds of times before, but August's words come back to me. Sex is supposed to feel good, isn't it?

Daddy holds my head and forces his wide girth deeper down my throat. I'm struggling to breathe, and my vision blurs as he grunts in pleasure with each push of his hips.

"Take it like the dirty cumslut you are," he says as he shoots cum down my throat.

I gargle, almost inhaling it up my nose, and swallow.

When he's finished, he grabs my hair and jerks my head back, leaving me spluttering and a trail of cum dripping down my chin. It'll hurt to swallow, and my eyes will be red for days, but this is only the start of what Daddy has planned.

"Follow me, Clementine," he says. He stops me as I try to stand up and pushes me back down. "Stay on your fucking knees. I didn't tell you that you could walk."

I crawl after him, conscious that August's cum is still leaking out of me and has dried hard on my inner thighs. When Daddy discovers it, being on my knees will be the least of my worries. The hard floor hurts, but I know better than to complain. Daddy pauses at the wall adorned with his unique toys. A shudder of dread trickles down my spine as he selects a leash and collar alongside an accompanying remote control.

"If you're going to be disobedient," Daddy says, kneeling and fastening the metal collar around my neck. It's tight enough to make me breathless but not enough to restrict blood flow completely. "I'll have to make sure you don't misbehave again."

"Yes, Daddy," I respond.

He walks quickly, too quickly for me to keep up. Whenever I go too slow, he presses a button on the remote, sending a jolt of electricity through me.

"Stand up," he orders.

I do as he says, wobbling and unsteady.

He grabs my shoulders and shoves me onto a nearby bed, like the ones you'd find in a doctor's office for female examinations. He ties my hands to my sides using restraints built into the bed and unclips the leash. He leaves the collar in place.

"Spread your legs for me," he says, grasping my ankles and putting them roughly into stirrups. He uses a strap to tie them there.

I'm exposed, laying open and bare.

There's nowhere to hide as Daddy stares at my wrecked pussy and August's cum filling me. He roughly shoves a speculum inside me. It's cold and uncomfortable, but he doesn't care as he cranks it wider to get a better look. I can't hide the evidence.

He shakes his head and exhales in disapproval.

"Daddy," I whimper.

"No talking," he snarls, silencing me. He grabs rubber gloves from a drawer, puts them on, and spends a few minutes probing my insides. "I can see what you've been doing, Clementine."

"Daddy, I can explain!" I plead.

"My friends were right about you," he says, taking off the gloves with a snap and hurling them across the room. "You're a dirty little slut who is desperate for cum. We agreed that you weren't allowed to fuck your pets, and without protection, you should know better."

My heart rate slows again.

"I'm sorry, Daddy," I say. "I couldn't help it."

It's the first lie I've ever told him.

"It's unacceptable," he says. "You've broken our rules. If you behave like a brat, I'll treat you like one. I've spoiled you too much, haven't I?"

"Yes, Daddy," I stammer.

"We need to get you all clean again," he says, then spits in my gaping hole, mixing his spit with August's cum. I get turned on by the sudden warmth and thought of the two people I've loved the most filling me with their spit and semen. "Daddy will need to teach you a lesson."

"Yes, Daddy," I repeat.

"But I'm not going to fuck you, Clementine," he says. "Your filthy loose pussy has already been used today. No, a girl like you must be taught a lesson you'll never forget. A lesson that will make you think twice before you decide to fuck your pets again."

He takes my feet out of the stirrups and uses the extra restraints on the bed to wrap around my thighs and tie my ankles, leaving me lying flat and spread open. He undoes the clasps holding my wrists at my sides and forces my arms above my head before binding my wrists together again and locking them to a chain. I'm completely immobilized.

Daddy enjoys controlling me. It gets him off. I used to enjoy his punishments. Sometimes I'd even break the rules intentionally. It's not the first time I would have fucked a pet to get at him. It used to be a game we'd play together, but this time feels different.

All that matters is that Daddy doesn't suspect August. He's happy for me to fuck his friends, but he wouldn't appreciate sharing me with his son. After August's repulsion when he walked in on Daddy testing his new toy on me, he would never suspect that August was capable of crossing the line either.

"I'll be right back," Daddy says.

He strolls to the special cupboard. It's as tall as me and where he keeps his prototypes. I'm always the first to try them. I don't have a good view from my position, but he takes his time to make his selections. In this part of the basement, Daddy's special playroom, there are no peepholes for August to watch through.

"This will do for a start," Daddy declares.

"What is it, Daddy?"

He doesn't answer but approaches me with scissors and cuts my slip down the middle. The fabric splits in a jagged line. When he's done, he grabs the material, bunches it into a ball, and forces it into my mouth.

"You lost the right to address me after you broke our agreement," he snarls, returning to the cupboard to retrieve his toys.

He twirls steel nipple clamps in his hands. My nipples have always been sensitive enough that I can come from gentle stimulation, but these clamps are going to take me beyond that point. Daddy is unapologetic as he clamps them on tightly. My nipples bulge as the blood rushes to them. They tingle and beg to be touched, but Daddy isn't going to satisfy me. He's already made that clear.

"You're not going to get a release," Daddy reaffirms. "Not unless I order you to. We could be here for hours."

Denying pleasure and robbing me of the sensations my body craves is torturous. I remember how amazing August's mouth felt latched on my nipples, and my clit swells.

Daddy hums, retrieving black tape and sticking it over my mouth, not caring that my hair is getting caught in it. The duct tape forces the slip deep into my mouth, but I can still breathe... just about. He then puts a black hood over my head. It has slits near my nostrils for oxygen, but I can't see. I'm entirely at Daddy's mercy.

Time stretches on for what could be minutes or hours, but he doesn't touch me. My nipples throb, and my skin prickles from his watchful gaze. Just as I'm starting to relax and think this may be my punishment, an electric shock to my nipples makes my body jolt.

Seconds later, an icy dildo forces its way inside my vagina. It feels like I'm being fucked by Frosty the Snowman. Daddy is being true to his word and not touching me, but I crave human contact. This is lifeless compared to August's hot throbbing cock that spilled his seed in me hours ago.

"Let that greedy pussy swallow it up," Daddy murmurs. "You like that, don't you, Flora? You like it when your body is fucking helpless and under my control."

My thighs clench.

Flora was my mom's name and hearing it is like a stab to the gut. Daddy continues to thrust into me hard. Suddenly, he pulls the dildo out. When I think he might be done, another giant toy pushes between my lips. I'm dripping, but it's so big that my pussy stings as it stretches to try and accommodate it.

"Good girl, Flora," Daddy says. "You're gonna take everything I give you."

When he's not happy, he calls me Flora. I'm not sure whether it's because he misses her or because he knows it annoys me. I used to get jealous when he called me Flora. My mom's the only woman he's ever loved. He's never had a girlfriend since. The only person he's fucked is me. I'm the last piece of her he has left, and I hate her for it—not because Daddy fucks me, but because he only fucks me because I'm part of her.

My body jolts as he rams the monster dildo in and out. It's not pleasurable. I only feel pain until I feel his hot breath against my clit. I wiggle and push my hips forward, but he laughs and slaps my clit hard. The sensation sends a tingle of pleasure through me. I want a mouth on there, licking and sucking until I come undone, but Daddy withdraws the toy again.

Footsteps walk away. The door creaks, then nothing.

My pussy drips over the bed and between my thighs, weeping August's cum like it was a mistake when all I want to do is hold it in there.

Tears fill my eyes behind the hood. I want to reach down and stroke the heat between my legs, but I'm suspended. I'm tied down until Daddy says I can leave. Panic rises in my chest as my breathing grows more ragged. The heat from having the hood over my face catches up with me.

How long will it be until he comes back?

Will I suffocate in here?

Daddy wants to teach me a lesson, I remind myself, not kill me.

Hours pass by, or at least I think they do.

It's not the first time he's punished me this way, but it's the longest it's lasted. Being alone gives me time to think about Daddy and everything he's done for me. He built my den for my special projects, shared me with his friends, and put my pleasure above all else... then, there's August. I'm drawn to him. I have been since we first met, but I can't have them both. My mind is a chaotic and confusing mess.

I concentrate and clench my pussy to squeeze my bladder. I desperately need to go to the toilet, but I can't hold it any longer. My cheeks flush with humiliation as I release, dousing my legs and the bed in hot urine.

A few minutes later, the door creaks open again.

Daddy has been waiting for me to break.

"Look at the mess you made," Daddy teases. I can't see him but sense his presence. "But you don't mind, do you, Pet?"

My ears prick up.

Pet?

I recognize Daddy's calculated footsteps, but a foul smell seems out of place in the sterile room.

Suddenly, the bed I'm tied to is flipped into an upright position. The restraints are strong and suspend me in the air like I'm on a fairground ride. My piss slides down and drips onto the floor, echoing around the walls.

"Your pet seemed so happy to fuck you earlier that I thought he'd like another go," Daddy says. "That's what dirty sluts like."

A yelp, a dragging noise, and another figure getting closer.

I try to move my ankles and wrists.

Daddy has punished me by withholding orgasms, but he's never humiliated me by bringing someone else in. He usually cares about ensuring I have a good time, but he doesn't want that now. That much I am sure of.

Daddy laughs as he sends an electric shock to my collar

and clamps, making me bite down hard on the fabric in my mouth. Reluctant surges of desire shoot between my legs.

"You will enjoy this, Clementine," Daddy hisses. "It's what you wanted."

He shocks me again. My trembling body breaks out in a cold sweat.

"Fuck her, Pet," Daddy instructs. "Show me how you fucked her earlier."

My pet sobs but doesn't make another sound as he approaches. How can he when his lips are sewn together? He's too much of a baby to scream and let the stitches tear. I've kept him for a few months. He is someone Daddy's friends wanted to disappear.

"I said, fuck her!" Daddy roars. "I gave you pills for a reason!"

The wilted head of a small cock jabs against my entrance.

"Fuck her like you mean it," Daddy snarls. "Harder."

The pet enters me and thrusts in short bursts.

Daddy can't see the tears running down my face. As much as I don't want this fucker inside me, my body is so grateful for finally being touched that it is responding like I've been taught. I don't want to come. Not for him. Please, no!

"Pets are not for fucking, Clemmie," Daddy says.

When the pet's cock is fully inside me, Daddy goes behind him and uses his body to push us closer together. Daddy bears down and forces him deeper until his sticky pubes touch my mound. The disgusting stench of the pet's breath seeps through the fabric and makes me want to heave, but I can't risk vomiting unless I want to choke to death.

The pet doesn't fight Daddy. He knows better than

that. Gargling sounds come from the pet's throat, and Daddy pulls off my hood. I gasp, pleased for the burst of air hitting my face, then my relief turns to horror.

Daddy's arm is wrapped around the pet's neck, holding him in a vicious headlock. The stitches on his lips start to rip as he cries out to resist. His eyeballs bulge as Daddy squeezes harder while his cock stirs inside me.

It's the first time I've seen this vicious edge to Daddy.

"This is what happens when you fuck without my permission, Clementine," he says. "I'm your Daddy, and you're my property. You'd better remember that."

The pet stops trying to talk as his face turns purple. After spending months with me, he's finally ready to welcome his death. He's lucky. If I were the one killing him, I'd drag out his death to prolong his suffering. Daddy's chokehold keeps the pet standing upright as his life drains away. Instead of his cock going limp, it gets harder as blood rushes to it.

"You're a twisted girl, Clementine," Daddy says. "Look at how wet you're getting. This is why you belong with me. I'm the only one who understands you. No one else can satisfy you like I can."

The pet's cock swells as he takes his final breath, and I gasp as his rotten cum releases inside me. There's so much of it. He fills my pussy with the life that's leaving his body.

"You're going to come, Clementine," Daddy urges. "Come for Daddy."

Tears of shame fall from my eyes as I shudder and come at his words. I can't help it. My body is programmed wrong. Daddy is right. I'm twisted. I'm wrong. I'm an abomination. When my orgasm is over, Daddy drops the pet's corpse in the puddle of piss at my feet.

"Maybe you'll think twice before fucking your pet

again," Daddy says, tearing the tape and pulling the slip from my mouth, making me cough. He pushes the bed back down until I'm horizontal and undoes my clasps, but I don't move yet. I can't. "If you disobey me again, it will be your life I'm taking as I fuck your sweet pussy."

CHAPTER 13

August

MY COCK TWITCHES AND MY BALLS ARE HEAVY AT the prospect of filling Clemmie again. Being inside her was even better than I expected.

I've been staring into the forest from the window for hours now. I expected her to return after she finished doing whatever she needs to do in the hellhole underneath the house. Dad got back hours ago. I didn't think anything of his early return, but now the sun is starting to set, and I'm getting anxious. There is still no sign of either of them.

Could she have told him what we did?

I wanted to show her that love could be special but was it possible to break a lifelong bond with a single fuck? It'd take time to show her how serious I am about what I said. I want a life away from here with her.

I leave my watchpoint and pace the mansion's corridors.

Why did this damn place have so many fucking rooms? It was easier when I lived in a trailer and could clear the space in ten steps. There are so many places where he could be keeping her and knowing there is a hidden lair beneath my feet doesn't make the search any more straightforward.

I stalk to the basement. As I do, my father approaches. He seals the basement door behind him using a ring on his finger. The fucker protects his sick, perverse world with his life.

My stomach churns. If Dad is sick, what does that make me? Am I as bad as him after what Clemmie and I did today? Do we have something in our DNA, some sort of genetic predisposition to be like this?

I grit my teeth and clench my fists. "Where is she?"

"You have a temper like your mother, August," Dad says. "I thought being here would show you that there is another way to behave instead of acting like an uncivilized animal."

As soon as I find Clemmie, I'll show him how an uncivilized animal acts.

"Where is Clemmie?" I ask again, not interested in playing his mind games.

"She has gone away for a while," he replies. "She left earlier, but she'll be back before your joint birthday party."

"Is she okay?" Panic rises in my chest like someone is crushing my ribs. "What have you done with her?"

He laughs and winks. "She's perfectly safe."

Okay and safe are not the same fucking thing.

"Is she still underground?" I question.

His eyebrows narrow in a furious line. "I heard about your outing this afternoon, and I trust you will stay quiet about what you saw. Who would believe you anyway? If anything, only one person would get the blame, and that'd be you."

He's right, and we both know it.

If cops come sniffing around and find Clementine's

playground, they would never believe a sweet innocent girl or my millionaire entrepreneurial father would be capable of committing a crime. I'm the one who would take the blame. The guy who grew up with a drug addict on the wrong side of the tracks is the obvious suspect.

"I won't say anything," I sneer, "if you tell me where she is."

"Blackmail." He rubs his chin thoughtfully. "Interesting. It's not what I expected from someone I took in out of the goodness of my heart."

"Why did you take me in, anyway?" I snarl. "Why not leave me to fend for myself? It's what I've been doing for years."

It's a subject we haven't properly discussed since my arrival. After Mom died, he was given the option of taking me in or letting me enter the system. He paid for a cab to drive me hours across the country, told me which room in the mansion was mine, gave me a truck to use, then we've hardly spoken since. I haven't stopped questioning his motivations since I set foot on the premises. He has zero to gain by me being here and everything to lose.

If it weren't for a pesky caseworker who persisted in speaking to me after Mom died, I wouldn't be here at all. Ironically, they start to follow up on their backlog cases when someone dies. Until then, I was another name in a dusty file they decided wasn't worth saving. But, without that interfering bitch, I'd never have met my Clemmie. I had no idea about her existence until I arrived, and she took my breath away. She still has it. After all this time, I'm still holding it in, and I can't fucking breathe.

"If you don't know why you're here by now, then you're not the person I thought you could grow to be," Dad says. "I shouldn't have to spell it out."

"Say it," I spit.

I have to hear it.

I've had my suspicions, but I needed him to say it.

"I need someone to take over," he says. "I need someone to look after this place when I'm gone. I thought my flesh and blood would understand better than anyone else. You're just like me, son."

"I'm nothing like you," I hiss.

He's a few inches shorter than me, and although he's gained a few extra pounds as he's aged, he's in good shape. There's also something intimidating in how he carries himself like he expects the world to bow down at his feet. In his world, everyone already does.

His eyes twinkle like we're sharing a secret. "We're more alike than you think."

"Bullshit!" I shake my head. "We are nothing alike."

"I see you, August," he says eerily.

His stare sends a cold shiver down my spine. For a second, it feels like I'm looking into a mirror at who I'll be in thirty years. I don't want his sick and twisted way of life. I want something better. I want to travel, get an honest job, come home to find Clemmie waiting, and fall asleep with her in my arms, happy that no one would ever hurt her again. He would never understand. How could he when he's used her as his pet for years, just like she is using hers?

I turn my back on him and storm away.

I want to shatter his fucking nose, but I can't do anything until I see Clemmie again. Dad is the only one who knows all the secrets hiding in the mansion. If there's a secret tunnel system, there could be another dungeon that I don't know about.

The crisp night breeze hits me as I step outside. My body buzzes from adrenaline, and I need a way to release it.

I put the key in the ignition of the beat-up truck I bought at the junkyard earlier with the wages I saved. It's our escape vehicle. I speed away, heading for the nearest bar and closest fight.

I don't know where Dad is keeping Clemmie or what she'll be going through, but I can't shake the feeling that it's my fault. He found out where she'd taken me, and now she's facing the consequences. Maybe my father and I are alike. Both of us like punishment, and when I get my revenge on him, I'll take great fucking pleasure in delivering it.

CHAPTER 14

Clemmie

THERE'S A SOUND IN THE DISTANCE.

"Daddy?" I call into the dark.

Nothing.

"Daddy? Is that you?"

How long have I been here?

Two days? Maybe three?

Besides Daddy bringing meals and removing the corpse, he hasn't spent any time with me. He doesn't speak or look in my direction when he visits. It's not the first time I've broken his rules, but this is different. I'm not sure whether my pet was the first person Daddy killed, but he blamed me for it.

I've never felt like a prisoner before, despite the chains and sex dungeon, but I'm starting to. I crave the freedom to feel the soil against my feet and the breeze running through my hair, but most of all... I crave August.

I miss him and our nights in the pool house. Thinking about him makes my pussy tingle and my dirty panties dampen. Will things be different when we see each other again after what happened between us? I hope so. The more time I spend here, the longer I have to consider his offer.

Being around August makes me feel alive, really fucking alive. The kind of alive I only thought I could feel when drawing a blade over someone's artery and watching their blood run until their heart stopped beating. I used to believe that collecting souls made me who I am, but he's changed that. He makes me feel whole. He's my other half, the better side of me.

I hope he's waiting.

My heart skips a beat at a crash on the other side of the door.

I jump and put my ear to it. "Daddy?"

"Clemmie?" It's August who answers. "Is that you?"

"August!" My heart sings. "How did you get in here?"

It must have been difficult for him to get into the basement, but he'll never get to the room I'm in. A retina scanner permits only Daddy to enter.

"That doesn't matter," he answers gruffly. "How can I get you out?"

"You can't," I reply matter-of-factly. There's a comfort in knowing he is a few inches away. Thankfully, Daddy didn't soundproof this private room. "Only Daddy can get in or out."

"Fuck," he curses. "But I've found another one of his rings, I'll—"

"Don't do anything stupid!" My voice rises a pitch higher than what is comfortable. "Daddy will let me out soon."

He pauses, then asks, "Are you okay? Did he hurt you?"

"He's teaching me a lesson," I reply. "It's nothing I don't deserve."

"I'm so sorry, Clemmie," August replies. His voice

sounds nearer as if he's sitting on the floor with his back against the door. "Is all of this because of what we did?"

I'm on full alert again.

"You didn't tell him, did you?"

"Fuck no," he says, "I just thought—"

"No, this is about something else," I interrupt, deciding he doesn't need to know the full details. I smile and slip back into our usual playfulness. "Have you missed me?"

"I thought he killed you, Clemmie." His words are loaded with deep intensity. "He said you'd be back soon, but I didn't believe him. I had to know for myself."

"We'll be together soon," I promise, "just like we were in the forest."

The silence stretches out. My pulse quickens, and I turn to put my hand against the steel. "August? Are you still there?"

I know he is. I can sense it.

"That's what you want, isn't it?" I ask. "You want us to be together forever, just like you promised."

"This whole thing is fucked up," he grumbles.

That's not a no.

"But you like fucked up, August," I remind him, thinking about how I trailed my fingers over his muscles. "You like us."

"We'll get out of here soon, Clemmie," August says. "This isn't the kind of life you deserve. We'll go somewhere out in the country. I'll fix up cars. You can eat, read, write, cook, and do whatever the fuck you want. I'll take care of you. I'll make sure you have everything you need. I'll never share you with another man again. Even your special projects and your pets—"

"I don't want to talk about my pets," I interrupt.

Daddy is treating me like I treat one of my pets, apart

from I have a small toilet and basin instead of a hole in the ground. My insides still feel tainted after my pet's final coming polluted me.

"What I mean," he continues, "is that I'll find a way. We'll make everything work, and I'll help you. Maybe, if you have the life you deserve, you won't even need them or your collection."

My collection is a product of years of hard work. It's been a labor of love. I've poured hours into making my artifacts: skinning bodies, teaching myself taxidermy, trying to repurpose a body and transform it into something else.

"My collection has been my life," I murmur.

"You can use those skills in other ways."

August keeps talking animatedly like a new life is viable, and we might have a chance at a future like the ones I've seen written in books.

"What if I'm not good at being normal?" I whisper.

I'm not sure whether he heard me through the door.

"I'll teach you," August says quickly. "I'll teach you everything you need to know. I don't know a lot, but I know how to take care of myself, and so do you. I'd do anything for you."

"Would you kill for me again, August?" I ask.

Daddy would, and I need to know whether he has what it takes. I have to be sure that we have a future together. One without secrets or pretending.

"Yes," he replies without hesitation.

"Tell me what you did to the cop."

August sighs but tells me anyway. "A cop pulled me over on the highway," he explains. "He was going to come to the party, but I made sure he didn't arrive."

"What did you do to him?"

"It doesn't matter," he says. "No one will ever find him

now, and no one will ever find us if we choose to leave either."

I giggle. "It's pretty hot knowing you've killed for me."

"You're fucking insane, you know that?" he jokes.

August sees me and accepts me. Something I thought Daddy did too... until he didn't.

"That's why you love me, isn't it, August?" I purr. "Because I'm not like other girls."

"No," he replies, his voice gravelly and deep. "You're not."

"I can tell what you're thinking about," I sing. "We have a special connection, remember? A connection that no one else can break."

"Tell me then," he challenges. "Tell me what I'm thinking."

"You're thinking about how good my pussy felt around your cock, and how much you wish you could be fucking me right now."

"You're wrong," he says. I imagine him pulling his sullen expression when he's trying to play hard to get. "I just want you out of there."

He isn't fooling me.

I remember his eyes gliding down my body, drinking me in like he wanted to devour me.

"Tell me what you'd do to me if you were the other side of this door," I say.

"This isn't the time, Clemmie," he warns.

"I've got nothing else to do," I reply, "Why don't you entertain me?"

"Clemmie." His voice is strangled, and I smile, knowing his cock will be rock hard. He's struggled to conceal his vast boner many times, and if his urges are anything like mine, I know that being in each other's company is irresistible.

"Tell me what you want to do to me, August," I demand as I start to touch myself. "I'm slipping my hand between my thighs now. I want you to make me come with your words. You said you wanted to teach me that sex is about connection. This is your chance."

"You're unbelievable, you know that?" I hear unzipping and know he's getting his dick out. I'd love to suck it, take his head in my mouth and lick it all over until he sprays his seed, and I can enjoy the salty taste on my tongue.

"Tell me, August," I say, sliding my finger down my wet slit. "Tell me what you'd do to me. I want to hear it. I need it."

"First, I'd ram my cock down your fucking throat so you can shut up with your whining and teasing."

"Uh-huh," I say, finding my clit and circling it. "I'd suck your cock so good, August. You know I would."

"I'd grab your hair and face fuck you until your jaw aches, but I won't finish," he says breathily. "When I'm done with your mouth, I'd explore your body. Fuck... I'd suck your perfect fucking nipples until your sweet little pussy is dripping. I'd want to make you beg, Clemmie. Make you moan and plead until you can't stand it anymore."

"Please, August," I whine, rubbing my clit furiously. "Please give me what I need."

"When you're begging," he continues, panting as he jacks himself off. Knowing he's pleasuring himself turns me on even more. "I'd taste you. I'd lick and eat your pussy like it's my favorite fucking meal. I'd hold your hips down and force you to take all the pleasure I can give. I'd coax your lips open and slide my tongue inside that wet tight pussy."

"Mmhhhhmm," I moan, massaging the wetness around my entrance but not going inside. Not yet. I imagine

August's head there and how good his hot tongue would feel exploring me. "How good do I taste, August? Tell me how good my pussy tastes."

"So fucking good," he grunts, "I could eat your pretty pussy for days. It's all I've wanted to eat since I first laid eyes on you."

"Really?" I gasp.

"Uh-huh," he says. He spits on his cock. "I've been watching you. Watching how your body has been begging me to fuck it, and I can't resist anymore. I can't hold back. I'd make you cum on my face, again and again, letting you squirt all over me until your thighs shake, and you're so wet that you're begging for my cock to fill you."

My heart races as I finger myself, feeling an orgasm build but holding onto it for the perfect moment. "How would you take me?"

"I'd grab your ass and guide your pussy onto my cock, then fuck you from underneath," he says. I imagine my tits bouncing against his sweaty chest and how his large hands would feel cupping my ass. I'd slide my wet cunt over him until I coat his balls in my wetness. "You'll be moaning my name, Clemmie. My cock fits so perfectly inside you; it's like we're made for each other."

"We are, August," I moan as he grunts, "we are made for each other. There's no one else more perfect for me than you."

My breathing grows heavier, and I throw my head back as I slip two extra fingers inside and succumb to the orgasm. They don't fill me the same way August would, but they help me ride the wave that's tearing me apart. I hear the motion of his hands working his shaft and quickening in pace.

"Fuck," he groans.

I imagine his cum exploding over his fist and think about how much I'd like to lick it off.

"August," I moan as my pussy squeezes tighter around my fingers.

Neither of us speaks for a few minutes then I hear him stand.

"I have to go before Dad realizes I stole the ring," he says. "I'll see you soon, Clemmie."

"Yes," I say, "you will."

The thought of seeing him again keeps me going. Even in the darkness, he is there with me. I'll think of him as I fall asleep. When I've upset Daddy before, it was just me with my thoughts, but I'm not alone anymore. August is with me. Wherever I go, he will follow.

I never thought I'd share a connection with someone stronger than the one I have with Daddy, but now... I can't stop thinking about life beyond the gates of the mansion, of life with August. Our garage. We could even find a way for me to fulfill my other urges. I know he'd do anything for me.

Realization dawns on me, and I see the difference between August and Daddy. They may share DNA, but they are opposites. August killed to save me, but Daddy killed to punish me.

CHAPTER 15

August

THE FUCKER RELEASED CLEMMIE FROM THE basement two days ago, but he's kept her locked in her bedroom since. I'm sure Clemmie's pet will have died from dehydration by now. Dad wants to keep her all to himself until our big birthday celebrations, and I haven't wanted to risk him catching us speaking as that could jeopardize my plans.

I've been meticulous in my preparations, and everything is starting to come together. I've had to act like nothing is wrong. I've made no adjustments to my behavior —generally staying out of my father's way, continuing to go to work as expected, and not asking about Clemmie. I need his focus to be on her today.

Whatever the sick bastard has organized for tonight will be nothing compared to what I have planned for him. I have it all figured out. The real question is whether Clemmie will forgive me when the night is over.

I head to her bedroom, knowing she isn't alone. Her cheerful singing of *Happy Birthday* comes through the wall. I knock twice.

"Come in!" Clemmie calls, and I push the door open.

She's sitting upright in bed and looks paler than usual. Her skin is almost translucent, but seeing her intricate veins remind me that her heart is still beating. That's all that matters.

Father sits on the edge of her bed, holding a giant cake on a platter. It is five layers high and slathered in pink icing with a ridiculous unicorn horn on top. Something you'd buy for a child.

"What do you think, August?" Daddy asks. He cocks his head to the side and winks. "Want a taste?"

My heart rate quickens. What does he know?

"You need to have a slice, August!" Clemmie insists. "Cake for breakfast is a birthday tradition in our house."

"You're both eighteen now," Father says. "It's a big day for you both."

"Where's my cake?" I hiss.

He laughs. "You'll get your present this evening," he promises ominously.

I don't want to know what he's planned, especially knowing his expectations for me.

Clemmie freezes for a split second but recovers quickly.

"We need to eat cake!" Clemmie announces.

"Patience." Dad tuts. "August needs to bring up an extra plate."

I grit my teeth, not wanting to leave them alone, but I do as he asks. My time of being compliant will end soon.

"I'll be right back," I say.

"Bring forks too, August!" Clemmie says. "I'm a woman now. Real ladies need to eat cake properly."

Dad's face falls. Is he questioning how long he can get away with passing her around to his friends? How old is too old for them? Pigtails, child's clothes, and a bald pussy won't fool them for much longer. Those animals can smell real jailbait a mile off. I race to the kitchen to retrieve the plates. The idea of eating cake with them is ridiculous, but I must play along.

When I return, Dad is sitting next to Clemmie. He has a fat blob of icing on the end of his finger. Clemmie's pointed tongue flicks out to lick it off, but he pushes his finger into her mouth, forcing her to suck it clean.

"Here's the plates," I say gruffly.

I want to rip his hand off his fucking arm.

"Come sit with us, August," Clemmie says, patting a space on her other side. "This will be my best birthday ever; I can feel it!"

Father's eyes dart to the cake knife in my other hand. "Why don't you cut us all a slice, August?"

A challenge lies beneath his words. I step forward and sink the knife into the soft sponge, releasing a sickly-sweet raspberry smell that turns my stomach.

"There," I say, slapping the cake down onto a plate for him.

"Today is only going to get better," Father promises, putting a mouthful of cake onto the fork and feeding it to Clemmie. "I've got you both something new to wear for the party."

My eyes narrow. "You want me to come to the party?"

Is it because he wants to reinvent me in his image or because he sensed something changing, in the same way a predator could detect when a threat is around? He can play God with Clemmie, but he can't with me. I'm his son and being a monster runs in the fucking family.

"Of course, it is your birthday party too," he says, ignoring my surprise. "I got you a new suit and a dress for you, Clementine. I'll leave them outside your rooms when it's time to get ready."

Clemmie claps her hands wildly. "I'm excited!"

"There you go," I say, pushing a large plate of cake into her hands to stop him from feeding her. As I do, my fingers brush against hers, and my cock hardens instantly.

Clemmie doesn't take small bites. She shoves it into her mouth, not caring about getting crumbs over her expensive sheets. Buttercream smudges above her top lip that I want to kiss off.

"Don't you want any cake, August?" Clemmie asks.

"I'm not hungry," I reply.

"A small piece!" she pleads. "Sit down and have one, please!"

"We should leave you to rest," Daddy says, standing and taking the cake with him. He turns to me. "Your sister needs to be ready for tonight, and so do you."

I nod abruptly and turn to leave. I may have a plan, but so does he.

"August?" Clemmie calls after me. I turn, and she grins; her entire face lights up. She really is an angel. "Happy birthday."

"Happy birthday," I mumble.

I'll make sure it's a birthday she won't forget.

CHAPTER 16

Clemmie

IT'S A GOOD THING DADDY TOOK THE CAKE AWAY. My stomach aches and feels like it's about to burst, but it was so delicious. It was the kind of cake that people dream about.

I'll spend the rest of the day making myself beautiful, especially now I know that August will be attending the party. I will take a long bath until my body smells of roses. No matter how often I exfoliate, I can't seem to get the rank smell of death out of my pores.

The tub is running when I hear a soft knock on the door. I pad out in my robe, expecting Daddy will have arrived with my new dress.

I open it partially and see August.

"August." My eyes widen. "You can't come in."

Not when Daddy's home. It's too risky. Daddy wouldn't like him in here unchaperoned.

August doesn't listen and steps inside. He puts his hand over my mouth. "We don't have long, so I need you to listen to every word I'm gonna say."

I nod.

I've never seen him this serious before.

"We're getting out of here tonight, Clemmie," he says with determination. "We're gonna leave that party together. Me and you, okay? I'm not leaving without you. We'll explore the fucking world just like we talked about."

My heart races.

August's eyes burn with a furious intensity that tells me he is willing to do anything. I see myself in him. I recognize the murderous rage, and it sends tingles to my pussy. August gets it. I see it now. He understands *me*.

When he reluctantly pulls his hand away, I whisper, "You're gonna hurt Daddy, aren't you?"

"Don't worry about what I'm gonna do," he says. "Focus on our new life together and leave him to me. In the meantime, pretend that nothing is wrong. Can you do that, Clemmie?"

I nod again.

"I love you, Clementine Jackson," August says, closing the gap between us. "If we don't leave tonight, he will find out and find a way to stop us, and I want you. I want you all to myself forever. Do you want that too?"

"Yes," I breathe.

"Good," he growls, taking my face into his hands.

His kiss steals my oxygen. I whimper in longing as his tongue plunges into my mouth, tasting me and taking my fucking soul with it. His hard cock presses against me, and I have to have him. He can't push me away without making a noise Daddy might hear. I paw at the front of his jeans, pulling his zipper down and tugging his cock free.

He holds my ass and hoists me into the air.

"After tonight, everything changes, Clemmie," he murmurs.

I kiss him hungrily in reply, never wanting this moment to end.

I let my robe fall off my shoulders and to the floor, leaving me naked in his arms and his cock sliding against my wetness.

"Shh," August whispers. "Don't make a fucking sound."

I sink my teeth into his neck to stop myself from moaning as his cock slips effortlessly inside me. His fingers dig into my ass as he uses me like a doll, sliding me up and down his shaft to claim me. He goes slow. We try to be quiet, but he gets excited. The wet slap of my pussy against his balls tips me closer to climax as he murmurs into my neck, "You're all mine, and after tonight, everyone is going to know it."

"I love you, August," I pant, then bite his shoulder as a surprise orgasm rocks my core and coats him in my desire. "I love you."

August's hips buck as he fills me, washing away and cleansing me of all the poison.

When I'm with him, everything is better.

My head spins as he withdraws and places me down gently, fastening his pants.

"Tonight will be the start of the rest of our lives," he promises, turning to leave.

"Wait!" I catch his wrist. "You said you were gonna handle Daddy, but what about the others?"

Sex has stirred another urge in me—a bloodthirsty one.

"What about them?" August asks. "We'll leave before the party starts."

"But what if we don't?" I slip my hand under his shirt and stroke his six-pack. "What if you leave them to me? Call it a birthday present?"

He freezes. "Is that really what you want?"

"Yes," I reply, staring up at him. "That's what I want."

This is how I'll know he truly accepts every part of me.

"Can you pull it off?" he asks.

I smile at the thought. "Of course."

I don't have long to plan, but I have enough time. Yes, plenty of time to get everything ready for the real celebrations to begin.

"Okay," he says after a few seconds. "But we go straight after?"

"Forever, August," I promise. "After that, we have forever."

SIX CARS HAVE ARRIVED. THERE ARE NEVER MANY guests. That's the point of my father's sick club. It's exclusive. It wouldn't be special if anyone could join it. I bet he has a waiting list of people who are dying to fuck Clemmie's sweet pussy. I know why he decided to keep her after her mom died. Every guest will suffer tonight, but none as much as *he* will.

Thankfully, the guests arrive alone without other kids. They wear expensive suits and shirts made from materials I can't pronounce. Their shoes are so polished that my spit would drip straight off them. Those men are wolves hiding in plain sight. They work in respected professions and are in positions of power: doctors, judges, and cops. All of them think they're invincible. They believe they can prey on the vulnerable and keep their perfect lives. It's how our world works, and my father is one of them.

I'll make *him* choke on his blood. I'll make sure there's enough blood to compensate for the amount of cum he's forced Clemmie to drink over the years. He'll regret his actions.

I put on my new pin-striped blazer. It fits me perfectly, and I fucking hate how it makes me look like him. I'm more comfortable in my work overalls and covered in oil. Father wants me to take over the twisted world he's created, but I'm going to take pleasure in watching his motherfucking empire burn. That'll be my lasting legacy.

I fasten my top button and straighten the collar. My white shirt won't stay this color for much longer. I make my way to the basement. Unlike last time, there is no security guard around to stop me.

It's odd to be on the other side of the wall. Men gather and drink by the bar, warming up. The air tingles with the nervous, excited energy of creeps getting ready to empty their tiny balls.

My father stands in the middle of them, playing the role of the perfect host. He knows how to manipulate people to get what he wants. It's probably how he made his fortune in the first place. A fortune that funded his sex toy side business and mysterious website. I wonder how much of his wealth was built on his talent or from exploiting the talents of others. Clemmie won't be the first person he's used.

"August." He waves me over and puts his hand on my shoulder. I want to shake him off, but I clench my fists instead. He introduces me to the group, "This is my son."

They nod in approval. I fake a smile, but it's unnatural and hurts my jaw.

"You're here for your birthday present, aren't you?" Dad says, then turns to others to add, "I promised him something special for his eighteenth. Something to turn him into a man."

They guffaw. A guest's dirty hand slaps me on the arm like we're old pals, and I resist the urge to break every bone in his wrist to stop him from touching any child again. I don't know what Clemmie has planned, but I hope she makes them all fucking suffer.

"Well, shit." Another grins widely, exposing his new veneers. "Look who has just arrived."

I follow their gazes and open mouths to see Clementine.

She glides into the room like a princess. She's wearing a white ballgown with a tight bodice and floaty skirt. I swallow hard as my heart skips a beat. She's stunning. She always looks beautiful, but now she seems otherworldly.

Her skin is flawless. Her eyelashes are black and thick, framing her sparkling green eyes, but it's her mouth that I can't look away from. Her pouty red lips could obliterate a thousand hearts with a smile. A smile that makes me want to tear out the throats of all the guys whose shriveled dicks are getting hard looking at her. She is all fucking mine.

"Darling," Father greets her, "why don't you make our guests comfortable? I'm taking your brother somewhere special for his birthday gift. I'll be right back."

"Of course, Daddy," she agrees as her eyes meet mine. I see a steely determination looking back at me. "I'll make sure our guests are comfortable."

"Good girl," Father purrs. The stupid fucker is oblivious as he turns to me, "This way."

I walk rigidly after him, ignoring every instinct telling me to stay by Clemmie's side. As much as I want to protect her, I need to trust that she can take care of herself. She kept a pet shivering and living in his shit, after all.

"Where are we going?" I ask as we pass through the sex floor. Clemmie's laughter gets steadily further away as I try to ignore all the toys mounted on the walls. There are hundreds of them. I don't want to think about how many of these he's used on my Clemmie.

"It's time I teach you the most important life lesson: how to be a real man," he says. "I need you to carry on our family business, August. I thought it was time for us to bond as father and son."

We head to the room where he kept Clemmie prisoner for a few days. It's his dungeon of sorts. His special personal playroom. There's only one way in and one way out. This is perfect, even better than my original plan to lure him upstairs.

He bends down, and a glassy panel scans his eyes.

The door clicks and swings open to reveal a trembling young girl staring back. The color drains from my face. We've never met, but she looks familiar; then I realize the obvious similarities between her and Clemmie. They have the same dirty blonde hair and similar green eyes, but this girl can't be older than twelve or thirteen.

Where did he get her from?

Dad claps me on the back in encouragement. "You can go first."

"Go first?" I stammer, needing to hear him say it.

"Fuck her, August," Dad orders. "Prove to me that you're a real man. Prove that you're my son."

The girl's shoulders shake, and snot drips down her face as she cries. My heart aches for her, imagining this is how Clemmie must have felt before he conditioned her to respond to his touch. But this girl isn't strong like Clemmie. Clemmie looks weak, but a darkness has grown inside her while she's lived in this place, allowing her to thrive in a twisted way. Her lookalike was likely abducted or sold into the hands of a monster.

"I-I-I..." I stutter, trying to lull him into a false sense of security.

"Don't make me regret this, August," Dad warns, his

voice a deep threatening growl. "I've brought you a virgin, and it cost me. They're hard to find at that age."

"How old is she?" I ask.

Dad ducks down to stroke her cheek. "Why don't you tell us, sweetheart?"

The girl cowers away from him, and I don't blame her.

She sobs harder, and he strikes her hard across the face, making her wail. "You answer when I speak to you."

"Twelve," the girl manages to say between hyperventilating.

She looks at me with pleading eyes.

I may not have been able to save my sister from his acts of depravity, but I'd make sure that this girl wouldn't befall the same fate.

"Move," I order my father.

He grins, misreading my request.

The girl starts backing up, shuffling away until her back hits the wall. I pursue her. She yelps as I kneel and stare into her face. She is terrified for her life.

"What's your name?" I say.

"Iris," she whispers.

"Well, Iris," I lean in closer and whisper in her ear, "I want you to close your eyes. Everything will be okay."

She sniffs and squeezes her eyes shut.

"Whatever happens," I say, "don't open them until I say so."

I stand and take my jacket off. Dad's judgmental glare burns into my back, analyzing every motion. His heady lust hangs in the air and gets caught in the back of my throat, making me want to be sick.

Iris pulls her quaking knees to her chest. I'm disgusted that her fear is down to me, but I'll make sure she gets out of here alive. Her and Clemmie. I can save them both. I don't know what happened between my parents, but I can only guess that what my mom suffered at his hands drove her down the path of self-destruction. This is for all three of them, but mostly it's for me.

I look back at my father. He grins in encouragement, the same smile that a doting parent would give a child participating in a race on sports day.

I roll my sleeves up slowly and purposefully, then I turn.

It's what I've been waiting for since the moment I arrived.

Dad doesn't see it coming when I smash my fist into the side of his face.

There's a loud crack, and I hope I've shattered his jaw. He staggers backward. He's unsteady on his feet but manages to stay upright. His fight or flight response kicks in, and he swings back. He would have been a match for me years ago, but his age and time spent indulging in depraved desires have given him a superiority complex. He thinks he's untouchable, but I can beat him.

"You're going to let her and Clemmie go," I growl.

"Is this what you've been waiting for?" he snarls. "To get me out of the way to take my place? To take Clementine and my money?"

"This isn't about money," I spit, diving forward and knocking him to the ground. A frenzy takes over my body as my fists act of their own accord. It's the same feeling that overpowered me when I killed the cop. "It never has been. You've ruined her life. What you do here, it's all fucking wrong."

Blood bubbles and spews from his mouth as the bastard laughs.

I pause, and he hisses, "Do you think you're any better

than me? I've seen how you look at her and how your cock gets hard whenever she walks in the room. I thought my gift today would help you. Give you what you want. She even looks like her. You can have this one all to yourself. She's unspoiled."

"You're even sicker and more delusional than I thought. Offering me this fucking child won't change anything," I snarl. "Clemmie's not spoiled. You are."

He tries to say something else, but I don't let him.

He wants to get into my head with his warped comments.

I'm nothing like him. I refuse to be.

I punch with full force again and again. His arms flail as he struggles, but he's not going anywhere. How many girls has he pinned down like this? How many times has he let his friends hold his fucking daughter down? He's not used to being defenseless. I take out years of pent-up fury and resentment until there's a toe-curling snap, and his neck twists at an unnatural angle.

I'd have been better off never knowing who my father was.

"Wh-wh—?" A tiny voice squeaks behind me.

My head jerks around to see the small girl watching through the gaps in her fingers.

"I told you to keep your fucking eyes closed!" I roar.

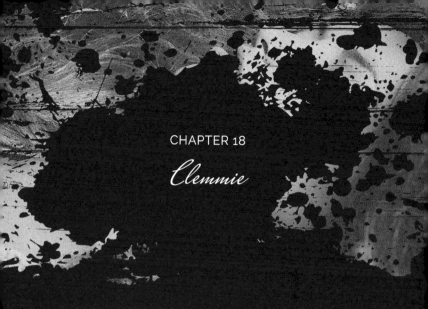

CHAPTER 18

Clemmie

"WHY DON'T I POUR EVERYONE ANOTHER ROUND?" I suggest playfully. "Shots!"

"Shots?" A regular chuckles, patting his round belly. "I think we're all too old for that."

Yeah, too old for a bottle of twenty-year-old liquor but not too old for me when I was twelve.

I pout and flutter my eyelashes.

"But it's my birthday," I say, running my tongue over my lips knowing they'll like it. "I'll make it worth your while."

"You heard her," another says as his slippery hand squeezes my ass. "Let's have shots for our pretty little lady on her special day."

I pour them double measures. This will be their second or third dose. I've overdone it to be extra cautious. I've never had so many pets to control at once. I can't take any chances.

I smile as they finish their drinks, and I stroll to the small stage. "Why don't I dance for you?"

They trundle after me like rats following the Pied Piper.

I've always liked the power I have over men, how I can manipulate them with the flick of my tongue or sway of my hips. I have something they want. Something they usually get to take, but not today. Today is different.

My time locked away has given me new bloodthirsty clarity. I've suffered at their hands, just like August said, and now they must suffer too. I climb onto the stage as the group lounges over the plush sofas. They don't know that the real show hasn't begun. When it does, the last thing they'll want to do is watch, but their limbs will be paralyzed.

"Why don't you all sing Happy Birthday to me?" I ask as I undo the zipper on the side of my skirt. I let it fall away and step out of it to reveal the rest of my gorgeous lingerie set underneath, complete with stockings.

I start dancing to the soft jazz in the background.

A man in the front row clutches his head and mutters, "I'm not feeling so good."

I close my eyes and focus on the music.

It won't be long now.

A glass slips through someone's figures and smashes.

Between grinding my hips, I watch as the men try to stand. A few take a couple of steps before falling and breaking their noses. I won't stop dancing until the song ends, busy thinking about what my life will be like soon. August and I. Together forever.

When the song switches, I survey the motionless group. Their limbs can't move, but they're fully conscious. My favorite. It's no fun when they don't understand what's going on. I don't want them to fight back, but I want them to feel every physical sensation. The greed and hunger in their darting eyes have turned to fear.

Daddy's parties have always been about *their* pleasure. I

obliged and believed Daddy when he told me it was an honor to be fucked by these prestigious men. He taught my body how to respond to them. He enabled me to feel pleasure from anything, and I let them take it from me. I'd spread my legs wide because that was my duty, but now August doesn't want to share me, and that part of my life is over.

August said I was his, and he was mine. The only thing I love more than August is feeding my urge to kill. I examine the limp bodies and consider the endless possibilities. There is so much potential in how they could be sewn together to make unusual statues, but I don't have the luxury of time. August wants us to leave tonight, and I have to be ready. But it doesn't mean I can't have a little fun.

I pull a knife from my corset and start singing, "Happy birthday to you. Happy birthday to you. Happy birthday, dear Clementine..."

Killing them will be the best gift of all.

CHAPTER 19

August

"Mister," Iris stammers. "Is he dead?"

"Yes," I reply with zero emotion.

My father's body is splayed at my feet. His features are unrecognizable. His blood has ruined my new suit, but I prefer it this way. Being beaten to death quickly doesn't seem like a harsh enough punishment considering his sins, but the real punishment is him knowing it was me who did it. His own flesh.

She swallows hard. "Are you going to hurt me too?"

"No, Iris. I'm not going to hurt you." I duck down to her eye level, but she doesn't meet my gaze. "No one is going to hurt you anymore. I want you to stay here and wait for an hour." I take the golden Rolex from my father's wrist and hand it to her. "When an hour has passed, leave the room and find a cell phone to call the police. No one else will bother you."

She nods shakily.

"Don't even think about coming out before then," I snarl venomously. "Or else."

She yelps and pure terror transforms her featu▓▓. Her

expression will be seared in my memory forever, but I know this is for the best. Guilt jabs my gut for having to scare her, but it's for the best. I need her to follow my rules.

I use all my strength to hoist Dad's body and stand him in front of the eye scanner to release me.

"Remember what I said, Iris," I say as I drop his body and use it to wedge the door open. "Give it one hour before leaving. Promise?"

"I promise." Her dirty hair hangs over her face. "Mister?"

"What?"

"Thanks for saving me," she mumbles despite her fear.

Maybe we could take her with us. I dismiss the thought before I can consider it.

I should kill Iris. I'm not a professional killer, but I know leaving a murder witness behind is rule number one of what not to do, but I can't bring myself to hurt her. That's the difference between my father and me.

"You're welcome," I say. "And if you tell anyone about what happened, I'll hunt you down and make sure the same thing happens to you, okay?"

I hate myself for it, but a threat could be the surest way to buy her silence.

She nods. "I won't tell anyone."

"Good." I smile, then tap my wrist. "Start the clock."

Before I leave, I spit on my father's body.

He can rot in hell.

~

I make my way back through the basement to the party... only it's already over.

Holy shit. My mouth falls open at the scene as I look around in horror.

The six guests lying around the room are in varying stages of undress. A man with a bulging belly and a back full of gray hair lies on his front like a beached whale. Another has his stomach ripped open and his intestines wrapped around his neck like a scarf. Next to him, a guy is crouched with a zebra tail coming out of his ass and multiple stab wounds to his back. On his left, a man's throat is slit, and his trousers are around his ankles. Both his testicles are covered in deep slashes, but the two who catch my attention the most are the two men Clemmie is still attending to.

A weird noise comes from one's throat like he's choking on his blood. He should be coughing it up, but he doesn't move. The white marble floor around him is covered in blood and looks like a contemporary art painting.

Clemmie laughs. Her beautiful, sweet laugh. She wags her finger at the choking man in disapproval. "You never said please before fucking me."

She pulls down his pants and grabs his wilted cock, grasping it hard in her hands. It turns red like an angry wrinkled raspberry.

"Clemmie," I call.

Every man watching this would want to hold their balls and run, but not me.

"August!" Her face lights up with glee. She's so happy to see me. She always is. "Watch this."

She takes the knife in her spare hand, holds the blade to his cock, then starts cutting through. The flesh splits as his blood sprays and covers her pretty corset. The guy pales as his eyelids flutter. He's not dead yet but will be soon.

"It's harder than I thought," she mutters in frustration

as she hacks his penis. "I thought it'd be easier because he couldn't keep it hard for long."

I watch, transfixed, as she saws through his penis like it's a piece of meat. My own cock isn't sure what to make of it. It winces at the thought of what's happening, but Clemmie's determination turns me on. She's sexy without meaning to be.

"There!" She declares, holding the stump in her hand like a trophy. "I knew I could do it!"

She stands and walks to the second man. She parts his mouth and rams the severed dick down his throat.

"How do you like sucking cock?" she counters, then laughs hysterically as we watch him suffocate to death. "Do you like deep throat?"

I find myself joining in and laughing at the absurdity of the situation. These fuckers deserve it. If they can't choke on each other's cocks, they shouldn't have made my sister choke on theirs. They've used Clemmie for too long. It's their turn to be her toys. I questioned her motives for keeping pets before, but now I'm starting to see that there may have been subconscious reasonings behind it.

Have her acts been about taking back control all along?

I gesture at the corpses and ask, "How did you do it?"

Clemmie is clever, but she isn't strong enough to overpower a group alone.

"I slipped tranquilizer into their drinks. I use it on my pets all the time," she replies, walking over to be at my side. "What do we do now?"

An icy chill runs down my spine at the sight of her beautiful blood-flecked face. The red spattering looks like freckles. Clemmie slips her fingers through mine and stands on her tiptoes to kiss me. She smells divine, like roses.

"We have to go," I say gruffly.

She looks down sadly at the guy with a cock in his mouth. "So soon?"

"Yes," I growl.

"Fine," she replies huffily, returning to the cockless man and plunging her knife into his neck to ensure his heart has stopped. "We can go now."

I pass her my suit jacket to cover her underwear as she tucks her knife into her garter. The sight of her drowning in my clothes, coupled with my adrenaline, makes my cock harden. As tempting as it is to take her, we'll have all the time in the world to fuck later.

She takes my hand, and we leave the basement. We climb the stairs to the first floor. As we reach the front door, I hear sirens approaching. Blue lights stream through the windows and fill the sky. The cars are hurtling down the drive toward us.

"August." Clemmie squeezes my hand so tightly that her nails will leave small half-moon imprints on my skin. "What are the cops doing here?"

Fuck. Fuck. Fuck.

We have no time to escape.

There's nowhere to hide.

"Clemmie." I turn and take her face in my hands. "You need to let me take the blame for this."

"But August..." Her bottom lip quivers. "We said forever."

"We are forever, Clemmie," I promise. "There's no getting away from each other. We're linked. Always. There's no tearing us apart."

"I can kill them, August," she says. Her eyes fill with tears. "I'll kill every last one of them."

There are five cars.

We stand no chance.

"You need to say I did this," I tell her firmly. "You're traumatized. I forced you to do terrible things. Can you do that?"

"But—"

"No!" I interrupt as brakes squeal outside. Howling sirens are so loud that it's hard to think straight. "Tell me you'll do that."

"I'll wait for you, August." She nods shakily. "We're forever, August."

"Forever, Clem."

I kiss her forehead as footsteps crunching in the gravel grow closer. I didn't want to ruin our final moments together by saying she would be waiting her whole life for me. Maybe we were never meant to be together at all. Perhaps this is *our* punishment.

The cops jump out of their cars, and the door flies open.

Guns point in our direction.

I push Clemmie behind me and raise my hands in the air.

"On the ground!" A voice yells. "Both of you."

I lower myself to my knees, and Clemmie does the same. Seconds later, the cops are on top of me. They haul me to my feet and force my wrists into handcuffs. I don't resist. They march me to a waiting car.

I turn back to see Clemmie wailing hysterically. Tears stream down her cheeks, making her mascara run as she sobs, "Thank God you're here!"

A female officer wraps her arm around Clemmie's shoulders and steers her away to another car calling for someone to bring a blanket. I breathe a sigh of relief. She isn't stupid.

I'm thrown into the backseat and look at her for the last time.

She's never looked more beautiful—even if she is covered in blood and wearing my jacket over lingerie. She is the perfect victim. My gaze looks beyond Clemmie to the mansion and at a small girl holding a cell phone in the window.

The car pulls away as Iris presses her hand to the glass, and I could have sworn I saw her mouth, "I'm sorry."

I wanted to rid the world of monsters, but did I become one in the process? Maybe it didn't matter, as long as she was safe.

AUGUST SHOULDN'T HAVE UNDERESTIMATED ME, nor should the foolish officers. They look at me and see an innocent victim. They don't notice the knife tucked into my garter as I'm ushered into the back of a cop car.

I cry hysterically, giving the performance of a lifetime.

I need to convince them if I'm going to fix this. I'm not ready for my new life to be over before it starts.

"It'll be okay," a female officer reassures, sliding into the back seat by my side. Two other officers sit up front, avoiding looking in my direction. They don't know how to deal with an emotional wreck like me. "You're safe now."

Safe? I want to roll my eyes, but I let the tears fall. The only place I'll be safe is with August, but they are tearing us apart. They want to split us up forever. The thought of being separated makes my chest ache like my soul is being ripped apart.

We start moving, leaving the only home I've ever known to follow the vehicle with August inside. It's the first time I've left the grounds in years, but it's too dark to see where we are. No other houses are around, and the road is empty apart from the car's tail lights ahead.

The other cops stayed behind at the mansion, undoubtedly fussing over the silly girl Daddy bought as a gift and the presents I left for them to find. I'd love to see their faces when they see my work.

"It's okay," the female officer says gently, patting my shoulder. "We won't be too long."

I have to act fast. There's no time to think.

I grab my knife in a smooth motion and slice it across her throat. Blood spurts from the open wound, and she gasps. Her hands fly to her neck in confusion, then her eyes widen as she realizes what I've done. She never saw it coming, and she'll bleed out soon enough.

The officer in the passenger seat in front turns around at the sudden commotion. The darkness is my friend.

"What the—"

Before he finishes his sentence, I launch at him with the knife, aiming for his temple. He tries to catch my wrist, but I'm quicker, and his head turning means the blade goes straight through his eye instead. That's more fun.

I pull out the knife and stab his neck to complete the job.

The driver realizes what's going on as blood sprays over the side of his face. He lunges to stop me but loses control of the car, and we swerve dramatically to the left. We veer off the road and hurtle down a slope. I'm bouncing in my seat but react fast and strap myself in. While the driver takes the wheel again, I lean forward to unclip his belt as he slams the brake.

The car halts, but his body keeps moving. He flies violently into the glass as we crash through the wooden gate, I brace myself as the wheels come to a natural stop. I'm winded but unharmed. Adrenaline will power me through. I can't stop now that I'm so close.

The other officers would come to our aid, right? People look out for each other in small towns, or that's how it seems on television.

While I'm waiting, I grab the female officer's gun and tuck it into my jacket. When animals were enough to satiate my appetite, Daddy took me hunting in the woods. I have good aim, and a knife wouldn't work in an ambush situation.

Smoke billows from under the hood as I stagger from the wreckage.

"Help!" I scream into the air. "Someone help us!"

Bingo! Just as I suspected, bright lights appear on the horizon as the car moving August loops back to the scene. They pull up, and their doors fly open. Suddenly, two officers are racing toward me, leaving August alone.

"You have to help us!" I screech. All of this fake emotion is hurting my throat. "They're really hurt! Please!"

They run down the verge past me to the car. As they do, I pass them and wait for the perfect moment. When they're at the car's windows, reaching in to help their colleagues, I stop and take my aim.

Bang.

One down. A shot to the shoulder. Not perfect, but it's enough to knock him over. The second officer is busy trying to haul a body out of the car. He has no time to draw his gun.

Bang.

My bullet hits him in the back of the head, and his brain explodes like confetti.

"Happy birthday to me," I sing as I skip down to finish what I started. I needed the keys to their car, after all. When

I reach the officer gasping for air, he's reaching for his walkie-talkie. I grin down at him. "You won't be needing that."

Bang.

Straight in the head. Bull's eye!

I find what I'm looking for in his pocket. There are cuff keys on his keyring. It must be fate. My plan couldn't have gone any better.

I make my way to August, who is trying to shoulder his way out of the locked car. He stops, and his mouth falls open as I emerge over the top of the hill.

"We said forever," I say as I open the door to release him. "I'm done waiting."

Authors Note

A huge thank you to my beautiful beta readers, Kyla and Ria. You guys manage to make my heart all warm and fuzzy, even when my books are about the darkest themes.

About the Author

Holly Bloom has a degree in English Literature, but don't let that fool you... she would pick a steamy romance over a Shakespeare play any day!

Holly writes contemporary romance - the dark, gritty and twisty kind. She loves creating badass babe characters, who aren't afraid to speak their minds, and writing about the men who can handle them - often, there is more than one! Why choose, right?

When she isn't working on her next project, Holly spends an unhealthy amount of time watching true crime and roaming around the woods near her home in the UK.

As well as gooey chocolate brownies, Holly's favourite thing in the world is hearing from her readers - her characters may bite, but she doesn't! Promise!

Find out more and sign up to Holly Bloom's newsletter to receive a free book at: www.hollybloomauthor.com

Printed in Poland
by Amazon Fulfillment
Poland Sp. z o.o., Wrocław

16322066R00089